TALES FROM THE SCAREMASTER™

HAUNTED SLEEPOVER

You don't have to read the

TALES FROM THE

SCAREMASTER™

books in order. But if you want to,
here's the right order:

TALES FROM THE SCAREMASTER

HAUNTED SLEEPOVER

by B. A. Frade
and Stacia Deutsch

Little, Brown and Company
New York Boston

Copyright © 2017 by Hachette Book Group, Inc.
Text written by Stacia Deutsch
Tales from the Scaremaster logo by David Coulson
TALES FROM THE SCAREMASTER and THESE SCARY STORIES WRITE THEMSELVES
are trademarks of Hachette Book Group

Cover design by Christina Quintero. Cover illustration by Scott Brundage.
Cover copyright © 2017 by Hachette Book Group, Inc.

Little, Brown and Company
Hachette Book Group
1290 Avenue of the Americas, New York, NY 10104
Visit us at lb-kids.com

First Edition: October 2017

Little, Brown and Company is a division of Hachette Book Group, Inc.
The Little, Brown name and logo are trademarks of Hachette Book Group, Inc.

The publisher is not responsible for websites (or their content) that are not owned by the publisher.

Library of Congress Cataloging-in-Publication Data
Names: Frade, B. A., author. | Deutsch, Stacia, author.
Title: Haunted sleepover / by B.A. Frade and Stacia Deutsch.
Description: First edition. | New York ; Boston : Little, Brown and Company, 2017. | Series: Tales from the Scaremaster ; 6 | Summary: "When their overnight class trip to the museum turns out to be more scary than sleepy, best friends Nate and Connor must stop a haunting—and the *Tales from the Scaremaster* book that seems to be pulling the strings—before they all become ghosts too" —Provided by publisher.
Identifiers: LCCN 2017004837 | ISBN 9780316438025 (trade pbk.) | ISBN 9780316438018 (ebook) | ISBN 9780316437998 (library edition ebook)
Subjects: | CYAC: Science museums—Fiction. | School field trips—Fiction. | Haunted places—Fiction. | Missing children—Fiction. | Friendship—Fiction. | Mystery and detective stories.
Classification: LCC PZ7.1.F7 Hau 2017 | DDC [Fic]—dc23
LC record available at https://lccn.loc.gov/2017004837

ISBNs: 978-0-316-43802-5 (pbk.), 978-0-316-43801-8 (ebook)

Printed in the United States of America

LSC-C

10 9 8 7 6 5 4 3 2 1

*Thanks to Jordan Apgar,
dinosaur expert, for all his help*

TALES FROM THE SCAREMASTER

HAUNTED SLEEPOVER

Don't make the same mistake
Nate and Connor made.
Don't read my book.

—The Scaremaster

Don't say I didn't warn you.

Chapter One

"Just five minutes," I said as I checked my wrist-watch. I know, no one wears a regular old watch anymore, but I like the way it ticks. "Come on, Mom, please. I want to look at a new book on *Ursus arctos*."

"Oh, I know that one!" My best friend, Connor Fletcher, was in the backseat of the car. He leaned as far forward as the seat belt would allow and said, "It's a kind of bird, right?"

"Yes," I told Connor, excited. "A massive black bird that has sharp teeth and can fly backward."

"Wow, that sounds scary—" Connor started, then stopped himself. There was a long pause, and then he said, "You're joking, aren't you? There's no bird that flies backward."

"Gotcha!" I laughed. "You're so easy to trick."

"I know." Connor sighed heavily. "My brothers tell me that every day."

I was an only child, but Connor's family was *big*. He was the youngest of four brothers. They all had the same dark skin, curly hair, and gray eyes. For a long time, his brothers had him convinced that his parents found him in the grocery store parking lot, until I stepped in and explained to him how genetics work. He looked too much like the rest of the Fletchers for the parking lot story to be true.

My wavy red hair was also a genetic trait. My dad was a regular brown-haired science geek. My mom was the redhead. I got the geek from Dad and the hair from Mom. Although Mom was a pretty big geek too. Nerdy genes ran strong in my family. And I liked that.

"*Ursus arctos* is the scientific name for a brown bear," I confessed.

Then I asked Mom again, "*Please?*" I tapped the face of my watch. "We don't have to meet our teacher for a whole half an hour. Can we go to the gift shop?" I added another begging "Pretty please?"

My mom was a librarian. It was hard for her to turn down buying a book. I had known that when I asked.

"Uh…" I could tell she was thinking about it

as she pulled into a parking spot in front of the Natural History Museum.

"We should get some candy to share with everyone at the sleepover," Connor suggested. "Maybe some gummy dinosaurs? We can identify each one before we eat them."

"Oh, all right." Mom gave in. "A bear book and some dinosaur candy. That's it."

I turned my head to wink at Connor. We were a good team. Educational gummy candy—that was a mastermind idea. How could she say no to that?

Mom handed me twenty dollars and said, "I'll bring in the duffel bags. Meet me by the ticket booth." She turned off the car engine. "Don't be late. Mr. Steinberg was very clear about the time."

I nodded.

Mr. Steinberg was our seventh-grade science teacher and the best teacher I'd ever had because he knew everything, kind of like a human Wikipedia. I wanted to be like him when I got older. Plus, he was also the one who had arranged tonight's sleepover in the museum for my entire class.

"We'll be there," I promised, taking one last look at my watch.

"Hurry," I told Connor, tugging his arm as he

got out of the car. "Every second counts!" We took off running.

Two minutes later, we were inside the Natural History Museum gift shop.

I'd been to a lot of museum stores, but this one was extra awesome. The shelves were packed with all the kinds of stuff I liked. Crystals, geodes, puzzles, build-your-own-dinosaur kits, boxes of fake bugs, dead butterfly dioramas, and books. Lots and lots of books.

If only we had more time. If only we could sleep in the gift shop instead of the museum!

I bolted straight to the bookshelf and found the book I wanted to buy. I'd seen it online when I'd looked up the museum and the exhibits. I knew exactly what the cover looked like.

I'd been to the museum several times before but always with my parents. This time it was going to be different. Mr. Steinberg was going to let us wander around, so I'd also printed a map of the museum and studied the guides to the most popular exhibits. I was 100 percent ready for the sleepover!

The heavy book had a big grizzly bear on the cover. Inside, there were "a thousand facts" about bears. That was more than any other book I'd ever read, but I had to make sure there was information in here I didn't already know.

Squatting on the floor, I flipped through the pages. On page 12, I found one thing I didn't know about bears. I'd already learned that it's sometimes hard to tell a black bear from a grizzly bear because both are brown. But this book said that grizzly bears have a shoulder hump. There was a picture of the raised part. There was also a picture comparing bear tracks.

This was definitely the book for me.

"Connor?" I called out. We'd separated at the entrance of the shop. He headed to the candy aisle, while I ran the other way.

"Over here," Connor replied. "You aren't going to believe what they have."

I hurried around a display of T-shirts and tote bags. I wanted to stop to look at the shirts, but Connor was waiting and I'd promised Mom. One book and candy. Nothing else.

"Check it out," Connor said, holding up a lollipop with a dead scorpion inside. "You're supposed to eat the bug."

"Gross." I stuck out my tongue. "Yuck."

"My brothers would love these," Connor said.

"Of course, they'd force me to eat all their bugs." He quickly put the suckers back on the shelf. "So, no thanks."

"Did you find gummy candy?" I asked, looking over the shelves of chocolate "dinosaur eggs" and licorice ropes that came with knot-tying instructions.

"Got them." Connor held up a big bag. The front said there were five types of dinosaurs inside.

"The brachiosaurus looks especially delicious," I said, taking the bag. In my head, I added up the prices and realized there was going to be some change left over. "We can get those licorice ropes too," I told Connor. "I want to make knots."

"Candy that comes with a book of instructions," Connor teased. "It's like it was made just for you."

I laughed.

We carried the candy to the counter, where an odd-looking woman stood at the cash register. There was no line. In fact, we were the only two customers in the store. And the woman didn't rush to begin ringing us up. She didn't seem to be doing anything except standing there, staring at us.

She was tall and thin and had long black hair, pale skin, and a narrow nose. But that wasn't what made her odd. It was her eyes. When she first looked up, I'd have sworn they were green, but a few seconds later, they seemed to be purple. I glanced away, and when I looked back, she was still staring at me, but now her eyes were brown. Every few seconds, they seemed to change color.

I elbowed Connor to see if he was noticing the same thing, but Connor was busy reading the little book that came with the licorice ropes. He hadn't looked up at the woman at all.

"Did you know the strongest knot is called a Palomar?" Connor said, pointing at an illustration.

"Those are best for fishing," I replied automatically, keeping my eyes pinned on the woman. Why hadn't she started ringing us up yet? "A figure eight is best for climbing."

"Show-off." Connor shut the book and set it on the counter. "We better pay and get going."

"That's what I'm trying to do—" I whispered, again looking at the woman, whose eyes were now yellow. "Um, excuse me," I said loudly and in my most polite voice. "We need to check out."

"Oh," the woman said, as if noticing us standing there for the first time. "I see...." She reached out for our purchases but stopped. "Do I know you?" she asked Connor. "Your face is familiar." She gasped, as if realizing where she'd seen him before. "Were you on the sleepover the night the boy—" Her voice softened, and in a whisper, she finished, "Disappeared?"

"Uh, I've never been here before," Connor told her. He looked scared. "But my brother Chris told me about the kid who disappeared."

"Such a sad story," the woman said, gathering up the items on the counter and scanning them at the register. "A real tragedy."

"I thought Chris was kidding," Connor told her. "It can't be true."

"It's true," she said flatly. A moment later, she spoke again. "We're out of bags. Wait here. I'll be right back." She walked toward the storage room at the rear of the store.

The instant the woman was gone, I turned to Connor. "What story? What kid?"

"Chris was messing with me at dinner last night," Connor replied. Chris was the oldest. Then came Charles and Cameron. Connor was last. Their parents had a weird love for the letter C.

Connor went on. "Chris said that he knew some-one who knew someone who knew the best friend of the sister of a kid our age who vanished from here during a sleepover."

"Vanished?" I repeated, wrinkling my eyebrows. "Like someone was kidnapped from the museum?"

"No. Not a kidnapping," Connor said in a nervous-sounding voice. "Cameron said that the exhibits in the museum are creepy and that the dead stuffed animals in the displays come to life at night. The animal spirits snagged this kid from his field trip. He was never seen again." Connor shivered, but not from the cold. "You know, there are predators like grizzly bears and T. rexes and lions in the exhibits, so maybe they ate the kid for dinner. No one knows what happened. But he was gone in the morning and never seen again. They didn't even find his body."

"Hmm," I said, considering the story but not buying it.

Connor also clearly did not want to believe the story, but I could tell that he wasn't sure anymore. He shook his head. "I told Chris it was bogus and that I wasn't falling for it. I was sure he was lying to try to scare me." His eyes widened, and he said, "But then a woman who works here says it's all true. What am I supposed to believe?"

Connor did not like scary stories. He hated scary movies. And he refused to read scary books. It would have been really easy for Chris and the other brothers to convince him not to come on the sleepover. One frightening tale about a missing kid, and Connor would have happily stayed home, safe in his bedroom.

"I'm sure it's one of those urban legends," I told Connor, putting a hand on his shoulder. "Your brothers are always goofing around."

"That's what I thought too, until now." He pointed at the cashier, who was coming back our way with a box of store bags in one hand and a leather book in the other.

"What if it's true?" Connor asked, his voice rising. "I can't spend the night in a haunted museum. I just can't."

"It's not true," I assured him. "Displays only come to life in the movies. And if there was a kid who disappeared in the museum, don't you think the school would cancel all field trips and sleepovers?" Like a lawyer, I added, "It would be a liability." I wasn't sure what that meant, but it sounded convincing.

"I guess, you're right," Connor agreed, though he didn't seem entirely convinced. "It's just a prank, right?" Before I could answer, he added, "But then again, how's it possible that the woman who runs the gift shop is in on my brothers' hoax?"

I didn't want Connor to get so scared that he'd leave and go home. "It's a coincidence," I insisted. "This is a classic museum ghost story. Your brothers knew it because they all did the sleepover when they were in middle school. Now this woman's tricking us too." I felt certain that was the truth. "I'll ask her. I'm sure she'll confess. Then we can all laugh about it."

The woman was back behind the counter. She had already put our purchases in a bag, and now she took my mom's money. It wasn't until after she gave me the change that I realized I didn't see where she had put the leather book she'd been carrying. It had looked cool from a distance. I'd have liked to check it out.

She placed our bag on the counter and said, "Have an interesting night."

Before she walked away, I asked, "Hey, about the missing kid story. It's a legend, isn't it? I bet it's something everyone who works here says to make the sleepovers more interesting, right?"

She turned away from me and pinned her now-hazel eyes on Connor. In a low whisper, she said, "The story of Blake Turner is absolutely true. His ghost haunts the museum."

Chapter Two

"Ha, ha, ha," I said. "Funny joke."

Connor looked sort of green and pale.

If he went home, it would be her fault. I wasn't leaving the store until she said, "Gotcha!" or whatever it was that pranksters in a museum say.

"It's true," she told us again. "I've seen him." Then she stepped away from the counter. Her back was to us, but I could see that she was putting something in a museum bag. There was no one else in the store, but maybe someone had called in an order. Since she was busy doing her job, I felt like I couldn't ask more questions.

I'd have to prove the story was a legend by myself.

"I think maybe I should take off," Connor told me. "I might have the flu." He coughed. "Let's go meet your mom, and I'll ask her for a ride."

"No, no," I protested. "There's no ghost haunting the museum."

First off, there was no such thing as ghosts, but I didn't argue about that. It's really hard to convince someone that something doesn't exist when they think it does. I've tried before to convince Connor that scary stuff in movies is created by writers, directors, and props departments, but he still gets scared. He's hopeless.

Instead, I said, "No kid named Blake ever disappeared from here. I'll prove it." I took out my phone. "Google knows all."

I was ready to do a quick search before we left the store, but when I looked at my phone, I didn't have any service. "Do you have bars?" I asked him.

Connor reached for his own phone. After checking that his phone worked, he asked, "What should I search for?"

"I'm not sure," I admitted. "Ghosts. Natural History Museum. Kid named Blake." I threw out words.

We were still standing by the counter. I looked out toward the main hallway, where we were supposed to meet my mom. I could hear voices. We needed to get out there, and Connor was typing and scrolling slowly, his face scrunched up in concentration.

"So?" I pushed Connor to google faster.

"Got it," he said, then took a deep breath. "Look at this!" Connor turned the screen so we could both see it. "It's true, Nate!" He started to read the print under the video: " 'A middle school student from Southside Junior High disappeared Monday night at the Natural History Museum. Blake Turner, twelve, was on a field tr—' "

"Nate! Connor! There you are!" My mother stormed into the gift shop. She was carrying my duffel in one hand and Connor's in the other. "What took so long?" She didn't pause to let me answer. "You were supposed to meet me. Your classmates are ready to start the tour. Mr. Steinberg sent me to find the two of you." She looked at the museum bag still on the counter. "Did you get what you needed?"

"Yes," I said. "We were just looking up… something…and got distracted."

"Well, you'd better hurry," she said, grabbing the bag off the counter. She set my duffel on the ground and stuffed the museum bag inside it.

My duffel was black with a green stripe. Connor's was the same but with a red stripe. We'd bought them together. She picked up my duffel, leaving Connor's on the floor. "Let's go, boys." She pointed at Connor, then at his duffel. "You can carry yours," she said with a grin. "What's in there, anyway? It weighs a ton."

"Pillow, sleeping bag, extra blanket, flashlight, heavy jacket and extra sweatshirt, second flashlight in case the first one doesn't work, and extra batteries in case that's the problem." It sounded to me like Connor had brought most of his bedroom. We were going away for one night, and he'd packed for a week. He went on, "Battery-operated reading lamp, water bottles, and a few comic books."

Yep, that was pretty much everything he owned.

Connor's brothers had probably helped him pack. They'd have pushed him to bring more and more stuff, laughing as he tossed in random things he'd never need.

Hefting his bag over his shoulder, Connor held out his phone toward me.

"We have to watch the video and find out what happened," he said, shaking the phone near my face. "And before your mom leaves, because once she's gone, I can't go with her."

"We'll watch it. Don't worry. What website is it on?" I asked as we followed my mom out of the store.

"I'll check." Connor looked down at his phone,

then realized he couldn't read, walk, and carry his heavy bag at the same time. "Let's put our stuff down first."

My bet was that it wasn't a real news site. His brothers had probably set it up. They would have known that Connor would find it. It was a bit unlike them to push a prank that far, but maybe they'd gotten frustrated that Connor refused to take the bait when they'd tried to scare him with the story in the first place.

We were just about to cross out of the shop doorway when the strange shop clerk called my name. "Nate?"

Had I told the woman my name? I didn't remember.

I turned back toward her.

"You forgot your package." She held out a museum bag.

"That's not ours," I said. "My mom took ours." Mom was too far ahead to stop and confirm, but I was certain I'd seen her put the bag into my duffel. One hundred percent sure.

"This belongs to you," the woman insisted. She held the bag out farther to me. Her eyes looked purple again.

"It can't be." I was going to refuse it again, but then Connor stepped forward.

"Your mom must not have taken the bag," Connor said, reaching the register in a few long steps.

"I guess…" I said, watching Connor stuff the museum bag into his own duffel.

"I've got it," he said.

That was actually a good sign. "Does that mean you'll stay? Now that you're the keeper of the candy?"

"Maybe." Connor lifted his duffel. "I want to finish researching the ghost first. Then I'll decide."

"It's fake," I repeated for like the zillionth time. "You have to stay."

"We'll see," Connor told me, holding his phone tightly, keeping the website open.

A cool wind seemed to blow from behind us as we were leaving the store. Chills ran down my spine. I looked back toward the counter, where the woman was standing, staring at me the way she had when I first saw her. She had a strange smile on her face. The corners of her mouth curled up, just a little, and her eyebrows pulled together.

I smiled back to be polite. Then I turned away

and hurried off to catch up with my mom before she left the museum.

There was a big pile of suitcases and overnight bags by the museum's registration desk. Connor tossed his bag on top and said, "Quick, Nate. We've got to watch the video."

Mom was talking to Mr. Steinberg, so I knew we had another minute. Everyone was greeting each other and chatting about the sleepover. I waved at our friends Bella Samson and Emily Vu and gave them a one-finger signal that meant we'd come hang out in a minute.

We moved to the side of the desk and put our heads together over the small phone screen.

Connor put in the password to unlock his phone. "Wait. What? This doesn't make sense," he said, scrolling through his open apps and pages. "Where is it?"

"Where's what?" I asked him.

"The story," Connor said, frantically swiping. "The video is gone. And the news site doesn't seem to have it anymore."

"Maybe someone took it down," I said, leaning in close over his shoulder.

"In the last three minutes?" Connor asked, still searching. He got very quiet. Then he said, "Google's got nothing anymore."

"That's because it never happened," I told Connor. "No story. No missing kid. You have to stay."

"I...I..." He kept looking for the story for another second and then said, "But where did the website go?" He raised his eyes to mine. "It has to be here." He kept searching, typing quickly and swiping his fingers over his phone's screen. "There's no way something was here one minute and gone the next. The Internet is forever."

"I bet your brothers did something to your phone. It must have been a made-up news story that they somehow planted for you to find when you thought you were searching the Internet."

Connor seemed to calm down a little bit as he considered what I said. "You really think so?" he asked.

I nodded. Because I did think so. Connor was right about one thing—Internet stories don't just disappear like that.

"Class!" Mr. Steinberg's voice echoed through the great hall. "It's time to begin our sleepover adventure." I looked over at our teacher. He was holding up a basket. "Place your phones in here. I'll give them back to you tomorrow afternoon."

Connor gave me a panicked expression. "I can't give him my phone. If my brothers did do something to my phone, I'll be able to find it. And if they didn't, well, then...I need to figure out what happened to Blake!"

Mr. Steinberg came to stand in front of us. "Phones, please."

I put mine in the basket and turned to Connor. "You've got to give it up," I told him. He was gripping the phone tightly in his hands.

"We're going to have fun. I promise. Just forget all about the stupid story."

"I don't know," he said, shaking his head, "I just don't know...."

"Come on, Connor," Mr. Steinberg said. "You're holding up the others."

"But..." He looked to me for help.

"It was made-up. It never happened." I told him, putting a hand on his shoulder. "C'mon, don't let this scare you. Stay the night. It'll be a blast."

Very slowly, Connor let go of his phone and put it with the others. His face looked like it had the night I told him we were watching a comedy and it turned out to be a horror. It was my April Fools' prank, but Connor didn't think the joke was funny. And now he was giving me that same suspicious expression.

"Pinkie promise," I said, holding up my little finger. "There are no ghosts in the museum."

He took a deep breath and linked pinkies with me. We shook them.

"I'm trusting you, Nate," Connor said.

"You'll remember this night forever," I told him, smiling hard. I was so glad he was staying.

We walked over to Bella and Emily.

"Where have you been?" Emily leaned in to ask me.

Before I could answer, Mr. Steinberg called for our attention.

"Say good-bye to your parents," our teacher announced. "It's time to begin."

Chapter Three

The planetarium show was honestly the coolest thing I'd ever seen. It was all about black holes. There were these awesome shots showing the death of a star. It was a little violent, dramatic, and completely epic. I also realized that I didn't know a lot about outer space. I was thinking I'd have to ask Mom to get me a book.

"Welcome to the dark side," Connor said in a low, rumbling voice. That was what the narrator at the beginning of the star show sounded like.

"I love the dark side," Emily said in a creepy voice as she walked between us. She had long hair that reached to the middle of her back. She pushed it forward to form a curtain in front of her face, and then she breathed through her hands to sound like Darth Vader.

Connor and I laughed.

We were walking out of the theater, down a

long, narrow aisle between the seats. Emily's family had membership passes to the museum, so she'd been there a ton of times. She'd seen the movie before too. "Did you feel it when the seats rumbled?" she asked us in her normal voice.

"That was the best part," said Emily's best friend, Bella, leaning over Emily's shoulder. The aisle was so narrow that the three of us barely fit across it, so Bella walked slightly behind us. She put her hands on my back and gave a small shake, just like in the beginning of the show, when we'd "blasted off" into space.

We stepped into a wide hallway in front of the planetarium. Our whole class was gathered there.

A few kids had to go to the bathroom before the next activity. While we waited, Bella said, "The planetarium has convinced me. I'm going to outer space." Her hair was as long as Emily's but twisted into two tight braids. She tossed her braids back, saying proudly, "I'll be the first black woman astronaut."

"It's a little late for that," Emily told her. "Mae Jemison was the first."

"Oh well," Bella said with a shrug. "I'll find something really important to be first at."

"President," Emily suggested. "You'd be a great president. I'd vote for you."

"Thanks. But I think I'd prefer to be an explorer," Bella said. "I could go under the sea or to the top of every mountain," she said. "Find somewhere that no one has ever gone."

"Send me a postcard," Connor joked.

Bella and Connor were opposites. Where he was afraid of everything, Bella was afraid of nothing.

While they talked about places Bella might explore someday, I wondered how Emily knew about Mae Jemison. I mean, she loved science and history, but so did I—and I'd never heard of Mae Jemison before.

"How'd you know about the first African American woman astronaut?" I asked her.

"Turn around," Emily said with a wink and a grin.

I rotated on a heel. Behind me was a picture of Mae Jemison and a little plaque that told about her.

"That's been here for years," Emily said, reminding me that she often came to the museum.

The seventh graders all came back from the bathroom break, and the museum tour officially began.

"This is a scavenger hunt," Mr. Steinberg said,

holding up pencils and sheets of paper. "You can go in small groups of three or four. You must stick together. And"—he pointed to a clock on the wall—"meet up by four o'clock, for snacks before our night health program."

A few kids clapped their hands. Most of us were looking forward to the health program. It was all about how the body works.

We got to choose our own groups, so mine included me, Connor, Bella, and Emily. We went to get the scavenger hunt paper from Mr. Steinberg.

"Have fun," he told us. "But beware of the bears." Our teacher pushed up his glasses and chuckled at his own joke.

"Everyone's a comedian these days," Connor said to me in a soft voice. "Mr. Steinberg sees them as stuffed bears in a permanent exhibit. He's probably interested in their habitat and boring stuff like that. But not me. When I see those bears, all I'm gonna do is wonder if they know anything about a kid named Blake."

"The kid never existed," I said. I'd been hoping that Connor had forgotten all about Blake, but unfortunately, that wasn't the case. I looked down at the scavenger hunt list. The first question was

"When do bears go into their dens to hibernate?" I was pretty sure I knew the answer, but going to the bear exhibit would be helpful.

"We get to go to the bears first," I told Connor. "We can ask them about Blake when we see them."

He wasn't amused.

"Want to take a shortcut?" Emily asked us.

The faster we finished the scavenger hunt, the more time we'd have to explore the museum on our own, so I said, "Sounds good. But could we swing by the room where our bags are?" I wanted my own map of the museum and the bear book I just bought. There were other maps available around the museum, but I wanted mine. I'd made notes on it of specific exhibits I wanted to see and some questions I had about them.

We made a quick stop by the luggage area. I went to grab my bag when Connor pulled his out instead.

"I took the bag, remember?" he said, pulling the museum shopping bag out of his duffel. "Let's just take the bear book," Connor continued. He was kneeling in front of his bag. "We can eat the candy at snack break."

"What candy?" Bella asked, excited. "My mom wouldn't let me bring any food."

"We bought a few things at the gift shop to share," Connor explained. He reached into the gift bag. "We got..." He pulled back his empty hand. Then Connor turned the bag so that he could look inside. "The candy isn't here," he said, looking up at me.

"Bummer," Emily said with a frown. "Do you think someone stole it?"

That was also my first thought. But no one in our class would steal from another student. No way. "Hang on," I bent down next to Connor, who was still hunched over his duffel. "It has to be there. Maybe the candy fell out of the bag?"

Connor shook his head. "No candy. And no bear book either." He pulled out what was in the gift shop bag.

"Whoa! It's that journal!" I exclaimed, recognizing the leather-bound book that the shop woman had carried out of the storage room. "She must have given us the wrong bag!"

I quickly went to get my own duffel. I'd been right all along: After unzipping it, I found the other museum store bag. "Here's our candy." I showed the girls the gummies and licorice. "And here's my book on *Ursus arctos*."

Connor looked as confused as I felt.

I kept the bear book and put the candy away, then sat down on the ground next to him. "Let me see the journal," I told Connor.

"I think we need to return it," Connor said, holding the book away from me. He sounded really nervous. "This isn't right, Nate. I can feel it."

"It's fine," I told him. I reached out and pried the journal from his fingers. "We can return it in a few minutes." I'd wanted a closer look when I'd seen it in the store. Now was my chance.

"Hey, Em," I said, glancing up at the girls. "Can we spare an extra five minutes? Will we still finish the scavenger hunt in time?"

"I know this museum like my own house," she said. "I'll get us anywhere, no problem." She sat down next to me on the floor. Bella joined us. We were in a circle around the old journal.

"What's that?" Bella asked me and Connor. She reached out and ran a finger over the rough brown leather. "There are these strange triangles etched in the leather," she noted, pressing into the gold lines that made each triangle. Bella pulled back her hand, saying, "I've never seen anything like this before. Where'd it come from?"

"No clue," I said. "The woman at the museum store gave it to us by accident."

"Or on purpose," Connor said, his voice in a near whisper. "Do you think my brothers set this up too?"

I quickly caught Bella and Emily up on the legend of Blake Turner.

"I never heard of anyone disappearing in the museum," Emily assured Connor. "And I'd know."

"Weird things are happening," Connor said, his voice trembling. "And I don't like it."

"It's just a normal journal," I told him. "Look." I flipped open the small brass latch on the cover and opened to the first page. "And it's blank."

The paper was thick and slightly yellowed with some stains and strange marks, but other than that, there were no words on the pages. I scanned through the first third of the book. Nothing. I went back to the first page and sighed.

"Boring," I complained. "For such a cool cover, I expected there to be something cool inside." I was about to close the cover and suggest we run it over to the museum store when, suddenly, Emily gasped.

While I examined the book, she'd been sitting next to me, twirling the pencil we'd gotten for the scavenger hunt. When I looked over at her now, she'd stopped twirling the pencil and was using it to point at the journal instead.

I followed her eyes back to the open page.

There was writing now.

It said:

Tales from the Scaremaster

Then, under that:

You think I'm boring?
Let me entertain you.

"Stop messing around, Nate," Connor said, a warning in his voice. "It's not funny."

"I didn't write that," I told him. "I swear."

"But there wasn't anything on the paper before." Connor scooted away from me and the book.

"Emily has our pencil," I told him. "Ask her."

"I didn't write that," she protested. "It's not even my handwriting."

Connor and I both quickly turned to Bella.

She shook her empty hands in front of her face. "Don't look at me. I didn't write in the journal."

I stared at the writing for a long moment, then asked Emily for the pencil.

Under the Scaremaster's sentence, I wrote:

We'd love to have you entertain us.

"No, we wouldn't," Connor said quickly. "No, no, no. We most definitely don't want the Scaremaster—whoever that is—to do anything with us." He stood up. "I have to go."

Bella grabbed his hand. "It's a book, Connor. It can't hurt us."

"Tell that to Blake Turner." He refused to sit back down.

"It's just a book," Emily assured him. "The writing must have been there all along and the pages were stuck together or something so we didn't see it. It's a gag. I bet your brothers are hiding out, laughing. I'm guessing they arranged this whole thing with the woman in the gift shop."

"If they wanted to scare me," Connor said, "then they've done a great job." He raised his voice. "Come out now. You got me. Ha, ha, ha."

His voice echoed around the halls, but no one answered.

After a moment of silence, I said, "The book is writing again."

I'll take you on a tour of the museum. You'll never call me boring again.

We all stared at the page.

"Okay, how did my brothers do that?" Connor demanded.

"It must be some sort of special ink. Or maybe this isn't a regular book with normal paper pages and there's an electronic component...."

The thing is, I couldn't explain how this was happening. But I wanted to find out. I wanted to let the book be our tour guide.

"What should we do?" I asked the others. "We do have an assignment we have to finish." I waved the scavenger hunt page.

"It's not graded," Emily told me. "Plus, you and I can probably get, like, ninety percent right without going to a single exhibit."

"I can help," Bella said, putting her hands on her hips. "I know stuff."

Emily reached out to her. "I meant all of us can answer the questions. Sorry, Bell."

"I'm not really offended." Bella laughed. "I say we do our best to answer the scavenger hunt questions and follow the Scaremaster to see where that takes us."

"I agree," I said.

"Me too," Emily said. She pointed to the page. "Nate, tell him we want the tour."

I raised the pencil and was about to write, when Connor grabbed the book. The pencil skipped across the page, leaving a long, squiggly line.

"No tour. No Scaremaster." Connor looked really upset now. "No weird book." He stood up and tucked the book under his arm.

We weren't fast enough to catch him. Connor rushed away from us and down a long hall.

I'd known Connor long enough to know exactly where he was heading.

He was going to the gift shop.

Connor was going to return the book.

Chapter Four

We caught up with Connor at the museum store. He was banging on the doors, calling out, "Let me in," and waving the Scaremaster's journal in his hands.

I reached out toward him. He flinched and moved away.

"This can't be happening," he told me, pointing at a sign on the shop door.

It said *Closed for Renovations. See you next week*.

I read the sign twice before I let it sink in. "Hmmm. That's weird for sure."

"You were in the store just a few hours ago?" Emily asked. "Weren't you?"

"Yeah." I told her that we had been the only customers. "So that's another weird thing."

"Maybe they were shutting down," Bella suggested. "You were probably the last people in there. That's not so strange. My mom's bakery will close for a few days sometimes to change equipment or get new furniture."

"It's a museum store," Connor exclaimed, banging on the door. "They don't have furniture or equipment."

"Maybe they're updating their computers," Emily offered.

Connor clutched the book to his chest and glared at us. "The Scaremaster closed the store. I'm sure of it." He thrust the book at me. "We're going to disappear, just like Blake."

I took the journal from him and for the first time noticed it had an odd smell. Like rusted metal mixed with wet sand. I've had tons of books and some of them have even smelled old, but I've never had a book that smelled like this.

"We aren't going to disappear," Emily assured him. I could see she was holding back a laugh.

"In fact," Bella added, "we're going to be the first ones to use the Scaremaster's journal as a guide and live to tell about it." She and Emily high-fived each other.

"Shh. Connor's too flipped out for jokes," I whispered to them.

My best friend had slid down to the floor and

was leaning against the locked shop doors. He had his head curled over his knees and was wrapped into a tight Connor-ball.

I sat down next to him on the cold tile floor. "Come on, man. You know this is all a trick."

He shook his head. "We're stuck with that horrible book."

"I bet you that your brothers are controlling the journal," I suggested. "They have to be. Wouldn't it be great to show them that you won't get scared so easily? This is your chance to prove you're not scared." Connor looked up at me, and I continued, "If you play along, they won't ever be able to bug you again. They'll know you're stronger than any prank they can play."

It was a good speech. One of my best. I looked over at Emily and Bella, who were both nodding in agreement.

Connor looked around the area where we were sitting. He whispered to me, "You really think my brothers are behind this?"

"Positive," I told him. "We've got to show them who's boss."

"I'm boss?" Connor said. It sounded like more of a question than a declaration.

"Yes, you are," I said, standing, then offering him a hand up. "I say we play along with the Scaremaster's book. Prove that we aren't afraid of anything. And then, when you go home tomorrow, you can proudly tell your brothers that they failed."

Connor took my hand. "I've got this," he said. "I'm not going to be scared. I'll show them who's in charge."

"Yes, *you* are," Emily said. She and Bella both hugged Connor.

"And we'll help," Bella added. She pushed back her braids. "Then, later, maybe we can come up with a way to scare them back."

From the look on Connor's face, I knew he liked that idea.

He took a deep breath and nodded. "I'm okay," he said, holding out a hand for the Scaremaster's journal. "I can do this."

I was so proud of my best friend. This was going to be a whole new beginning for Connor. Now we could finally go trick-or-treating. We could see movies that weren't animated. We might even be able to play the *Zombie Hunters* video game together.

Now that Connor was in, I did have one important thing to tell my friends.

"I really want to do the class scavenger hunt first," I told everyone. "I know it's not graded, but I bet Mr. Steinberg will expect us to know a bunch of information that you can only find out from the exhibits. I think we should do the scavenger hunt and then take the Scaremaster's tour after snack break."

"Ugh, you're such a nerd," Bella said with a snort. "We need to follow the journal now. What if"—she glanced at Connor—"his brothers go home?"

"We have to take that chance," Emily said, agreeing with me. "We're starting late, but we should do the project. Nate's right. We can't skip it."

"I really don't think it's a big deal," Bella argued. She looked at Connor, but he just shrugged.

"Let's ask the Scaremaster," I suggested. "That way"—now I looked at Connor—"his brothers can go get a snack and meet up with us later."

Emily handed me back the journal. That metal odor I'd noticed had faded. It was all musty sand now. Like the beach or a sandbox.

I opened to the first page and found that our conversation was still there. Under his promise that we'd never call him boring again, I wrote:

must do school stuff first. can we meet up for the tour later?

The Scaremaster replied right away:

After tonight, you won't need school.

I rolled my eyes and laughed. "Sounds exactly like something Chris would say."

"Yeah," Connor said, getting into it. He took the pencil and the book from me.

We'll meet you at midnight.

"That's after lights-out," I told Connor. We were supposed to be in our sleeping bags at eleven sharp. "*You* want to sneak out from the sleeping area?"

Connor smiled and gave me the pencil. "It's also the time when Chris and Cameron watch their favorite TV show. They don't ever record it to watch later. It's on tonight, and they don't miss it." It was a sci-fi show about aliens. I knew because I watched it too, but I wasn't as crazy as they were about seeing it on time. Connor's brothers didn't want to see spoilers online by accident.

"It's got to be midnight," Connor said defiantly. "Let's mess up their night. Chris and Cameron will be bummed."

"Way to take control," Bella cheered, offering Connor a high five. They slapped palms.

Must be midnight.

I wrote that just to be perfectly clear.

We gathered around and stared down at the book.

Do not be late. Prepare to be scared.

I'd have thought that last line would have freaked Connor out again, but it didn't. "Yeah, whatever," he said out loud, as if his brothers could hear through the book. "Hey, bros, you're the ones who are gonna miss your TV show. Too bad for you!"

He was met by silence.

The rest of the afternoon crept by. We finished the museum scavenger hunt.

We didn't have time to go back to our bags to get the candy, so we snacked on the carrots and hummus that were available to everyone. After snack, we had a discussion with an expert on biology. It was a great discussion, and my nerd cells were partying hard by the time we ate dinner. After dinner, we were given free time to walk around in the health exhibit. Connor, Bella, Emily, and I used some of that time to make our plans for after lights-out.

Finally, we said good-bye to the girls, and headed over to our separate sleeping areas. Connor and I settled into our sleeping bags.

All the stuff we had seen was really amazing, but I'd had trouble concentrating. I must have checked my watch two hundred times. There were 3,600 seconds in every hour. The ticking of my watch marked each one. It was painful.

After lights-out, I passed the minutes reading

the bear book with a flashlight I'd borrowed from Connor. So that I wouldn't get caught, I was way down in my sleeping bag with my head covered. That made my watch's ticking even louder, which made time pass even more slowly.

Finally, it was ten minutes to midnight. It was showtime!

We were on the second floor of the museum. The girls were sleeping in the health exhibit area. The boys were in a room filled with old pottery. We'd had such a busy day that everyone on our floor seemed to be asleep already. At least, no one moved when I stood up. If anyone was awake, they probably thought I was going to the bathroom.

I hoped it was also quiet in the girls' area. I didn't want to get caught. We'd get in big trouble if we were caught. I was trying not to think about that.

The plan was for all four of us to meet up in the front hall, right by the registration desk.

"What's in the bag?" Connor asked me as we tiptoed past a large clay pot and into the next room, which was filled with crystals and minerals in glass display cases.

I was carrying the museum gift shop sack because I didn't have my backpack with me on this trip. In it I'd put the things I thought we'd need for our adventure. My museum map. The Scaremaster's journal. A pencil. The flashlight I borrowed from Connor. And the candy, in case we wanted to snack on something during our Scaremaster tour.

"Give me the dinosaur gummies," Connor said, his hand out. "I wouldn't want you eating them all without me."

I laughed quietly and handed them over. "But I'm keeping the rope licorice."

He stuck the bag of gummies in the big pocket at the front of his sweatshirt and patted the outside. "Now they're safe."

We went down a large central staircase to our meeting place.

"Hey," I whispered when we caught up with the girls.

"Hey," Bella whispered back.

We didn't want to talk loudly in case our teacher was patrolling the halls. So I held up the book and Connor's flashlight. We gathered around it.

The Scaremaster wrote:

44

We begin in the Hall of Birds.

"I know where that is." Emily pointed the way. It was upstairs on the fourth floor. We tiptoed up the broad main staircase in the central hall and then took another staircase up two floors. We didn't dare use the elevators because they'd make noise.

Emily led us through the Hall of Reptiles and Amphibians and into the birds' room. We'd been here on the scavenger hunt. There were large glass windows with displays behind them. One was set like a desert, with mountains and birds placed around the scene, as if the birds were alive and enjoying their habitat. The displays were a lot like dioramas we made in elementary school, only way bigger and way more awesome.

For the scavenger hunt, we'd had to answer a question about how king penguins carry their eggs. The answer was on a plaque by the display: The eggs sat on their feet.

We stopped by that plaque, and I opened the Scaremaster's journal, wondering what he'd show us on his special tour.

Some birds eat seeds.
Others eat insects.

Go to the third display on the
left side.

We did.

It was a display of birds of prey.

I wasn't worried about talking out loud now. We were on a different floor than our snoozing classmates, teachers, and the few parents who were staying the night as extra chaperones.

"Birds of prey are pretty cool," I said.

The display was packed with hawks, falcons, eagles, vultures, and some others that I had to read the plaques below them to identify. When it came to science, I preferred mammals. Birds weren't really my thing.

Emily put her hand on my arm. "I've been here so many times. I've never noticed all these birds in one display case," she said. "Usually the displays break up the scenes by geographic location. Like, they might put certain kinds of hawks in California, and since some vultures live in Africa, they'd put them in another case."

"It sure is crowded in there," Connor said. He poked his finger at the display glass. "There must be thirty birds, maybe more."

Since the Scaremaster was our guide, I figured he could explain what we were seeing. I wrote:

Why are all the birds of prey together?

It seemed a basic question a museum escort would know.

He answered:

Wait and see.

I didn't know what that meant.

I showed his reply to the others.

"No clue what he mean—" Emily began, when suddenly, a loud screeching sound came from inside the display case.

I looked to see that rats, maybe ten or fifteen of them, were scampering across the floor of the display. The birds, which I swear had been dead and stuffed, began to circle, swoop, and screech. It was a battle for which bird could capture which rat. The rats spread out, dodging the birds. The birds swooped down, coming at them from every direction.

"I can't look." Connor closed his eyes. "Run, rats, run."

"The birds aren't real," Emily insisted. And yet, they were going crazy, swooping and squawking. "The rats aren't real either," she added. "This is a museum, not a zoo."

"Seems like a zoo to me. This is the stuff that happens after hours when the guests go home." Connor peeked through his fingers, then covered his eyes again.

Bella, Emily, and I couldn't look away. It was like a strange, terrible show, and we wanted to see it to the end.

I thought it was over when the rats disappeared. It looked like they had all discovered safe places to hide. We never saw any get caught. But the birds weren't happy. In fact, they seemed furious. And hungry.

A big black vulture with white-tipped feathers noticed us standing there, watching. With a resounding *whack*, the vulture hit the glass.

Connor jumped back.

The other birds decided that the vulture was onto something, and they began hitting the glass as well. Small cracks began to form in the large display window, stretching from the spot where the birds were attacking toward the edges of the frame.

"They're going to break through! Connor shrieked. "We need to run!"

"They're not real." Emily held her ground, refusing to run away.

I agreed with Emily, but as more and more birds charged at the glass and the shattering lines seemed to be growing, I agreed with Connor too.

Bella, being the boldest of us all, stepped toward the glass for a better look. "They sure do seem real," she said. A hawk slammed into the window right in front of her. "Hmmm. I saw a movie like this once," she added calmly.

"I saw that one too," I said. "The birds attacked the town." I held the shopping bag in one hand and the journal in the other. I gave Connor's flashlight to Emily. "Real or not real, it doesn't matter anymore. We need to get out of here!" I yelled so I could be heard over the birds' squawks.

"Head back in the direction we came from," Bella said, pointing toward the reptiles' room.

I made sure Connor was with us. If this was a

trick by his brothers, they'd honestly put a lot of thought into how to scare him. He probably wouldn't sleep for a week. Then again, I had no idea how they'd done this. It seemed way too life-like. But now wasn't the time to figure it out. Now was the time to run, which we did.

As we reached a display of frogs, I heard the distinct sound of glass shattering behind us.

"The birds are loose," Connor cried. "They're going to attack us. We have to hide."

"They're fake," Emily shouted back at him. "Your brothers did this, remember?"

Connor didn't answer. It was going to be hard to convince him that his brothers were still behind all this. It didn't feel like a movie or animatronics or computer holograms. It felt real. And pretty terrifying.

I was going to grab the map from my bag to pick a safe spot to hide, when an eagle flew into the hall we were in. Its wings were outstretched as it soared over our heads. I'd never seen an eagle so close-up. Its talons were so big—and sharp! And the beak looked like it could tear us apart.

"There's a bathroom at the end of the hall," Emily told us.

"Everyone run for it!" Connor called as he bolted down the hall.

I got to the bathroom second, with Emily right behind me. It was the girls' bathroom, but that wasn't a concern as we looked for a place to hide.

"Hold the door shut," Connor said, panicked. "Don't let the birds in."

We stood against the door. Something slammed into the hard wood a few times, and then the hall outside fell silent.

"Whew," Connor said, slumping over a sink. "That was close."

"It wasn't close," Emily said, though I thought I could see fear in her eyes as well. "It was fake." The more she said "fake," the more I felt that she wasn't sure.

A chill swept up my spine as I realized something important.

"Where's Bella?" I asked the others.

"I thought she was ahead of me," Emily said. She called for Bella, then ran stall to stall, kicking in the doors. They were all empty.

"We closed the bathroom door after Emily came inside," I said.

"I thought Bella was here before me. I swear I

looked back and didn't see her behind me," Emily said.

"I can't remember if she was even with us in the amphibian room," I admitted. My brain felt cloudy.

Connor stared at us eyes wide. "Are you still thinking this is a prank?" he asked. "Because I'm thinking *not*."

There was only one way to find out what was really going on.

I opened the Scaremaster's journal and wrote:

where's Bella?

There was no answer.

I wrote it again:

where's Bella?

This time, the Scaremaster wrote back right away. It said:

I love grizzly bears, don't you?

Chapter Five

Emily hurried outside the bathroom, shouting, "Bella! Bella! Where are you?"

There was no reply. The halls were eerily quiet. No birds screeching, no rats scuttling, nothing. Not even an air-conditioning fan.

Connor and I stood together by the bathroom. My heart was beating in my head. "Bella must be in on the joke," I told him. I took a few deep breaths. This was insane. I did not believe that some possessed book had sucked up Bella.

"This is probably what happened to Blake." Connor breathed the name as if it were too scary to say out loud. "I bet the Scaremaster took him too."

"No way," I said firmly. "That story isn't true. This is a prank." I was resolved to stay calm until we had evidence one way or the other.

"Bella doesn't even know my brothers," Connor said. He shook his head. "I was going along with you until we got attacked and Bella vanished. Now I know the Scaremaster is to blame."

Emily rushed over to us, frantic. "We have to find Bella." She was no longer saying everything was "fake." She was concerned, but she was also focused. "Even if she's hiding, we have to find her." She turned on Connor. "Tell your brothers this is not funny. Not even a tiny bit."

Connor's eyes were wide with fear. "I don't think they're doing this. Let's go get Mr. Steinberg," Connor said. "We need help."

"We don't have time for detours." Emily pointed at the Scaremaster's journal in my hands. "He says we go to the bears, so let's go." She raised two crossed fingers. "Hopefully, that's where she is."

And with that, we were off.

I swear I was practically running down the hall. I was worried about Connor. I didn't know if he'd pass out from fear, run back to the bathroom to hide, or go downstairs to find our teacher.

Connor was like a jittery tour guide as we crossed through different rooms and exhibits on the way to the bears. "Are those butterflies moving?" he asked as we crossed through the hall and into the spiders' room.

I liked spiders, and this area hadn't been on the scavenger hunt. Under normal circumstances, I'd have lingered, but Emily was yelling, "Hurry up!" and Connor was shouting, "They're going to get me!"

Finding Bella was way more important than seeing samples of the nine hundred different kinds of spiders in the museum.

Maybe once we saw that Bella was safe, hanging out in a back room watching that sci-fi show with Chris and Cameron and whatever techy friend of theirs who'd set up this whole Scaremaster adventure, we could come back.

North American mammals had a special hall on the far side of the insect displays.

I never saw any of the butterfly or spider displays moving, but I'll admit that when we passed a bighorn sheep diorama, I thought I saw one of the sheep tip its horns at me as I passed by.

Impossible, I told myself. This whole Scaremaster thing was getting to me. There was no way that every display was moving. Even if Chris and Cameron spent weeks preparing for the fake bird attack, they couldn't have also rigged every butterfly and spider and bighorn sheep display.

We passed bison, moose, and jaguars before reaching the bears.

Connor continued to report that every animal was moving, but I figured fear was making him see things.

The grizzly bear on display was the same as the one on the cover of the book I'd bought. It was huge and brown and standing on its rear legs as if ready to attack. The book had taught me that the difference between the grizzly bear and a regular brown bear was the hump on its back. This bear had a mighty hump.

The display was of the grizzly in tall grass. A sign nearby said the habitat was designed to look like Kodiak Island in Alaska.

"Bella, come out now," Emily called, her voice echoing in the narrow hallway. "Chris? Cameron? This isn't funny anymore. Send her out."

There was no answer.

Emily turned to me. "I'm starting to freak out a little."

"We'll find Bella," I assured her.

"Where is Bella?" Emily said in a soft but firm voice, leaning slightly toward me, as if trying to communicate directly with the leather journal.

I opened the book. The Scaremaster hadn't written anything new. The last sentence told us to come to the bears. That was all.

"Just like Blake," Connor muttered under his breath. "It's happening."

I needed Connor to relax. Emily was on the edge of losing her cool, and his talk about Blake wasn't helping.

"Calm down," I said to both of them. "Bella's probably hiding out around here, ready to jump out and scare us. Then we'll all laugh."

"I like that idea," Emily said. "I can't wait to laugh." Her hand was shaking when she pointed to the book. "Ask the Scaremaster."

I opened the journal.

I wrote:

We are at the bears. Where is Bella?

The Scaremaster replied right away:

Who is Bella?

"That is not funny." Emily snatched the book out of my grasp.

"Hey," I protested, but she held out a hand to me, silently asking for the pencil. In that moment, Emily was scarier that anything we'd seen in the museum. I gave her the pencil.

She wrote so fast that her usual neat handwriting was a mess.

> *You told us to come here to find Bella, and we did. Now, where is she?*

Inside.

"That's it?" Emily asked, staring down at the page. "Inside what? Inside where?"

I didn't know. I repeated what I thought and had told her before. "Bella's inside some back room, where she and Connor's brothers are peeking out and laughing at us."

"No," Connor said. His voice was soft, steady and light like a whisper. "That's not it."

"What do you mean?" I asked, turning to him. "Do you know where Bella is?"

His breath caught in his throat. I stared at him, standing there with his eyes open as far as they could open and his jaw slack. His skin looked like someone had covered him with chalk.

"What is wrong with you?" I asked. When Connor didn't answer right away, I followed his eyes to see what he saw in the grizzly bear exhibit.

I saw the bear, but it looked just the same as when we'd entered. It wasn't like the brothers had used their animatronics or holograms to make it move.

Around the bear, the grass was still. Mountains with snowy caps were painted on the back wall. Inside the display were a stick and a rock and behind those...a boy.

A boy?

Yes. I was sure I was now seeing what Connor saw. By the side of the diorama, in the farthest corner, there stood a boy.

I glanced at Emily. She was seeing him too. She

reached out and took my hand in hers. I gave it a squeeze.

The three of us stood side by side. The boy stepped forward and stared at us through the glass.

"That's not Bella," I said, as if that might break the moment.

The boy moved past the bear, straight up to the glass, and put his hands on the inside of the window. We could all see him clearly now. He was about our age. Shaggy dark hair and a few freckles. He was wearing gray sweatpants and a red baseball jersey with the number twelve on it. On his head was a matching baseball cap.

The hat said "Wildcats" on it. That was the mascot of the middle school across town. We were the Trojans, and our biggest rivals were the Wildcats.

"Is it possible?" I wondered out loud, peeling my hand away from Emily's and stepping forward toward the glass.

The boy in the display case at first looked as solid as the rest of us. But as I stared deeply at him, I could see a shimmer around his edges, as if his clothing and skin were blurry on the sides.

"Is that a ghost?" Emily asked me.

"Maybe." I shrugged. I really didn't know. Maybe we were looking at another hologram. I sure hoped so.

It was Connor who dared to ask the question. "Who are you?" he shouted to the glass, though by his voice, I could tell he already knew the answer. He was just asking for confirmation.

The boy moved his lips, but we couldn't hear him.

Emily moved to the glass. She banged her hand on the window.

"Where is Bella?" she demanded, overemphasizing each syllable so the boy could hear her clearly.

He had a sad, sorry look in his eyes as he glanced to the side of the display area, out of the frame to the left.

We couldn't see what he saw, but whatever it was, it made him step back, shaking his head. It seemed to me that he was trying to stop whatever would happen next.

He shook his head again. Then he looked at us with an apologetic expression. Like, "Hey, I tried...."

I was trying to piece everything together, but my head was spinning. I had no clue what was real and what was my imagination. I couldn't decide whether we were still being haunted by Connor's brothers or by an actual ghost. Was the Scaremaster really pulling the strings of our night? I was trying to put together a puzzle that was missing large and important pieces.

Suddenly, the bear in the case growled. Seriously. It was like when the birds started moving, only this time it was the bear. A huge, mean grizzly bear. The sound filled the display case and bounced off the walls in the hall where we were standing. The bear dropped from his hind legs to all fours and started to prowl forward.

"What's going on?" Emily cried. "Who's that kid, and where is Bella?"

The boy glanced quickly over his shoulder at the bear, then tipped his head repeatedly to the side, as if trying to tell us something.

"There's a door," Connor said, showing us a brass handle that glimmered in the hall security lights. "He wants us to go through the door."

I was surprised that Connor had gotten all that from the head tipping, but sure enough, it seemed to be what the boy wanted.

The bear was pacing behind the boy in the case. The boy didn't seem scared, but rather irritated at all the growling and snapping of jaws. The bear's grizzly fangs were dripping with saliva.

A thought flitted into my mind: Could a bear attack a ghost?

Wait. No. Why was I even wondering that? There were no *real* bears in the museum. No ghostly boys existed. Then again, that bear looked mad, and it was stalking along the glass window. I didn't want to have another incident like we'd had with the birds.

"He wants us to go through the door," Connor repeated himself, a little louder this time.

"Okay," Emily said, deciding for us all. "That must be where Bella is, so come on."

I didn't know what to think.

It was Connor who convinced me. "Let's go," he said.

"Huh?" I turned to him. The bear was now slamming his paws against the glass window, and like before, small fractures were appearing in the glass.

"It's not my brothers playing a game. It's the Scaremaster's story and we're in it," he said, his voice serious. "I'm tired of being afraid. There's only one thing to do. We have to find Bella and beat the Scaremaster with our bravery."

"Wow," I said, impressed with Connor and willing to follow him into battle against his fears... and mine. But he was right. What choice did we have?

"Let's go," I agreed.

We were pleased to find the unmarked door was unlocked. Connor took the flashlight from me and was about to plow forward into a long dark hallway.

"Hold on," Emily said. "Connor, who is that ghost?"

"It's Blake Turner," he said. "The boy who disappeared."

Chapter Six

It felt a little like Connor and I had switched places. He was brave and ready to face the Scaremaster head-on. I was ready to throw the book into the bear diorama and let the grizzly rip it up.

Science was no longer helping me. I was starting to face the fact that some supernatural things existed, things that two hours ago I'd have insisted were impossible. With every step farther and farther into the hidden areas of the museum, I was becoming more and more convinced that we were following the actual ghost of a kid who'd disappeared on his field trip. And with every step, I worried that Bella, or one of us, might be the museum's next ghost.

The hallways behind the exhibits were a perfect place to disappear. They were like a labyrinth. I felt sure there was a light switch somewhere, but we didn't know where it was to turn it on. Our only light was the thin beam from Connor's flashlight.

Ghosts glow in movies usually, but in real life, they don't.

Connor shined the flashlight, alternating between the floor where we were stepping and the space ahead. He'd flicker the light to catch the back of Blake, who was moving fast ahead of us.

The main corridor, where we were walking, branched off into smaller and even darker hallways every few feet.

In my head, I imagined the people who had installed the exhibits carrying materials, decorations, and wall plaques through these large, secretive passages. They'd create new dioramas and special exhibits. It made me feel better to think that the staff all arrived safely at their destinations. I mean, no one talked about museum staff disappearing. Who'd risk their life to work here? But then again, none of the employees were being guided in these hallways by a ghost boy and a possessed journal.

I tucked the journal into the shopping bag and slipped it under my arm. Then, in the darkness of the passage, I reached out to take Emily's hand on one side and Connor's on the other. We needed to stick together.

We moved slowly. Occasionally we'd lose sight of Blake, but then he'd stop and wait. His expression was impatient.

"He wants us to hurry," Emily told us. "We have to walk closer to him."

After several turns, we found ourselves in front of a wooden door carved with a detailed triangle design.

"Can I have the flashlight?" I asked Connor, feeling the hairs on my arms stand straight up as goose bumps traveled down my skin. He gave me the light, and I shined it at the door. Then, with a sharp breath, I pulled the Scaremaster's journal out of the bag.

I held the book under the same light.

"The triangle pattern is the same," Emily said with a gasp. "What does that mean?!"

"I guess we're on the right track," I replied, feeling a little hopeful.

"Where'd Blake go?" Connor asked, looking away from the door.

We looked around for him and realized that ghostly boy had vanished.

"We're going in," Emily announced. "Blake must have gone through the door."

"Through?" I asked, even though we all knew we hadn't seen this strange door open.

"Through," Connor echoed. He reached out to the knob. It was a tarnished, plain silver ball. "It's unlocked," he said, "just like the one by the bears."

He pushed open the door, and I flashed the light in before we crossed the threshold.

"It's a storage room," I said, feeling a little less scared. It wasn't like anything in a storage room might attack us. Right?

Connor found the light switch.

Bathed in florescent light, this room was not scary at all. But Blake was nowhere to be found.

The room had all the normal signs of human life. There were plans on the walls for new displays and bookcases stuffed with the kinds of books I loved to read: science, history, and anthropology.

In the corner were boxes marked "Costumes—India."

"That's for a new exhibit opening next month," Emily said, peeking in the top box and lifting a red silk scarf. It had fine gold embroidery along the side. "Ooh, pretty," she said as she set it back. Then, as she closed the box lid again, Emily screamed.

"What?" I cried out as Connor and I dashed across the room to her.

"There." She raised her hand to where Blake was now standing near the door we'd come in. In the light of the storage room, he seemed more transparent. I could actually see the shadow of the wall behind him.

Blake had his hands behind his back.

Connor and I went to stand with Emily.

"He popped up out of nowhere," she told us. "That's what scared me."

"No kidding," I said. "Me too."

Emily glared at Blake and said, "Stop doing that. It's not nice."

He raised his eyebrows and grinned.

Blake hadn't spoken, and I wondered if he could. He was standing by the carved door, still holding his hands behind his back. He looked like any other middle school kid, one that we might be friends with.

I decided to try a conversation.

"Blake?" I asked. I felt silly. Like I should be on some paranormal TV show. The kind of show I never watch.

He nodded.

Before I could say anything else, Emily jumped into the conversation. "Where is Bella?"

Blake lowered his eyes away from us and very slowly brought his hands out from behind his back. He was no longer smiling. In his hands was one of Bella's tennis shoes.

"No!" Emily screamed, lunging forward to get the shoe. As she flung herself toward Blake, he stepped back through the carved door, dropping the shoe as he went.

"He has her," Emily shrieked. She pulled open the door, stepping out into the dark hallway. "Connor, give me the flashlight!"

He quickly handed it over, whispering to me, "Emily's scarier than the ghost."

"I know." It made me laugh, but just a little. Everything else was a nightmare. How did Blake get Bella's shoe? Where was she?

Emily swung the beam of light into the hall, and we were all surprised to find Blake standing there, not too far away.

"S-S-Scaremast-t-ter," he said, stuttering the word out. This was the first thing he'd said since we'd "met."

"Scaremaster what?" I asked as I grabbed the

book out of the bag and fumbled around in the bottom of the sack for a pencil.

He pointed at Emily, who was the closest to him.

"Maybe he's asking us to ask the Scaremaster where Bella is," she said, pointing a long finger between Blake and the book.

"We already asked him," I said, "And that's how we ended up here, chasing a ghost."

"Just do it, Nate," she said as she wrinkled her forehead. "I think I'm starting to understand Ghost Boy."

Blake frowned.

"We've asked the Scaremaster about Bella before," Connor echoed me.

"Ask again," Emily said. "Ghost Boy wants us to."

"Bl-Bl-Blake." The ghost pointed at himself. He was clearly struggling to speak.

"Right," she said, turning her gaze from him to me. "He doesn't like being called Ghost Boy."

Blake gave a nod and a small smile. He pointed at the book again, shaking his finger.

"I'm on it," I said, turning to the first page.

Connor and I were in the storage room. Emily was in the hallway a few feet from Blake, shining Connor's flashlight at his face.

I wrote:

Where's Bella?

The Scaremaster wrote back:

Want to hear a story?

I looked at Blake. He nodded.
I wrote: **Yes.**
There was a pause while the entire Scaremaster book seemed to reset. The page cleared and all the writing, both his and mine, disappeared. Then, a new heading appeared:

Tales from the Scaremaster

Once upon a time, there were four friends on a sleepover at the museum. Bella and Emily both disappeared....

"Huh?" Connor looked to me. "That can't be right."

I read the page out loud again.

"That's what the story says," I told him.

We felt the cold wind at the exact same time. It blew through my hair, and Connor wrapped his arms around himself.

Slowly, very slowly, we both looked up. We knew what had happened before we even saw it.

The hallway was dark.

Blake had disappeared.

Connor's flashlight was sitting on the floor. The beam was pointing at the wall.

And Emily was gone.

Chapter Seven

I officially freaked out.

Connor, on the other hand, was completely chill. I don't know if it was the shock or what, but he was calm and in charge.

"The Scaremaster cannot scare me," he declared in a strong voice. I couldn't believe this was the same Connor who had almost backed out of the sleepover because of a creepy story.

A creepy story that turned out to be true.

"Well I'm pee-in-my-pants scared," I said, not ashamed to admit how scared I was. "What are we going to do?"

Connor took the Scaremaster's journal from me. "We have to get our friends back," he declared with determination. "And Blake's going to help us." He tipped his head to a spot over my shoulder.

I twisted around and looked up to discover that Blake was back in the room.

"Can you talk?" I asked the ghost.

He shrugged but didn't say anything. I considered that he'd been alone, wandering the halls with just the animals for friendship all these months. Maybe he hadn't spoken in such a long time, he didn't know if he could say more than a few words at once.

Clearly he wasn't willing to try.

Blake pointed at the book.

Connor sounded 100 percent confident when he said, "So far the Scaremaster has mostly acted like a museum guide, but the book is called *Tales from the Scaremaster*. We just have to have him tell us the whole story about us, and then we have to figure out how to tack on a rescue scene at the end."

It sounded like a good idea. "When did you get so smart?" I asked Connor, giving him a wink.

"About three minutes ago," he replied.

We sat on the floor of the storage room. I placed the book on the floor between us. Blake hovered in the corner by the door. He was obviously curious but didn't come close to us.

When I opened the book this time, I was surprised to find that an entire story was written there. Scratchy writing filled the whole page.

"Read it out loud," Connor told me. He closed his eyes to concentrate. "I'll work on the ending."

Tales of the Scaremaster

Once upon a time, there were four friends on a sleepover at the museum. Bella and Emily both disappeared....
And soon Connor and Nate would join them.

At that part, I looked up wide-eyed at Connor. "Go on," he said.

I went back to reading.

The story didn't tell us anything about where the girls were or what it meant that Connor and I would be soon with them. It turned out that most of the story wasn't about us. It was about Blake, who slowly moved closer as I read the tale.

Blake Turner was a shy, unhappy boy.

The Scaremaster changed his life.

I glanced up at him. Blake's face didn't register emotion, but he was listening intently.

Blake came to the museum on a field trip but lagged behind the rest of the group during the tours. He wasn't friends with the other kids. He didn't make friends easily; he never knew what to say when he was in a group. So he hung behind the others, listening to the guides and studying the exhibits.

A few days earlier, Blake's parents had announced that they were going to move to a new house. When he got back from the field trip, they'd start packing. It wasn't fair. They'd only recently moved into this house. He was going to his fourth school in two years. Blake didn't want to move and start over again.

At midnight, while the other kids slept, Blake stayed awake. He got up and slowly wandered the halls of the museum.

He met the spirits that lived there.

The bears, the spiders, and the birds were kind to him. They wanted to be his friends.

Standing in front of the grizzly bear display, Blake made a wish.

He said it out loud: "I want to
stay in the museum forever."

The Scaremaster heard Blake's
wish. He made that wish come true.

Now Blake lived at the museum
with the animals.

And yet, it wasn't the happy
place Blake had imagined.
He was lonely. He was sad.
And he wanted a friend.
A human friend who was
his own age.

When another school tour came
to sleep at the museum, Blake
realized that there was
something better than having

one new friend. He could have
four new friends!

That was where the story looped back to the place it began:

Bella and Emily both
disappeared... and soon Connor
and Nate would join them.

Under that was one final sentence:

Blake and his friends lived
happily ever after.

The End

I took a deep breath. "Wow." I glanced up at Blake. While it did seem kind of cool to live in the museum, there's no way I'd pick that over my normal life. Plus, I wouldn't want to be a ghost. I'd never make the same wish.

"You chose to live here?" I asked him.

Blake cleared his throat. His voice came out in

a squeak as he said, "Yeeess," then more firmly, "Yes."

"Come on, Blake. You know we aren't staying with you forever. You have to let us go." Connor closed the Scaremaster's journal and handed it to me. "Where are Bella and Emily?"

Without another word, Blake raised his feet off the floor and floated out through the carved door. A moment later, he popped his head back into the room. His voice was getting stronger and clearer as he gave us instructions.

"I'll show you, and then maybe you'll want to stay," Blake said. "Follow me."

Connor and I exchanged a look. "This might not be a good idea," I warned.

"It's all we've got," Connor said. "We have to find our friends and end this story once and for all."

I put the Scaremaster's journal in my shopping bag and flicked on Connor's flashlight. We'd need it again as we followed Blake's ghost down the winding halls behind the exhibits.

"I'm ready," I told Connor as he opened the door to the storage room. "Try not to disappear." It was a lame attempt at a joke.

Connor raised an eyebrow. "Ditto."

Laughing made it all just a tiny bit less scary, but I had one big thought that I couldn't shake off. While Connor's idea to change the end of the story was good, what if it was impossible?

If the Scaremaster wanted us to become ghosts in the museum, I didn't think we could stop him.

We wove our way through the dark hallway.

"I think this is the way we came," I told Connor. "It feels familiar."

We were walking side by side. He was close enough that if he started to disappear, I could grab him. And him, me. I wasn't even sure what disappearing might feel or look like. The girls were there one second and gone the next. But if there were a way to keep Connor with me, I'd do it.

"We can't be going the same way," Connor said. "Didn't we turn left last time?"

"We just turned right," I said.

"These passages are super confusing in the dark," Connor told me.

I still had that museum map, but we hadn't needed it while Emily was with us. Now I thought it might be handy. Of course, if we stopped we might lose track of Blake. So we went on, following the flashlight's beam and the outline of Blake up ahead.

When Blake disappeared through a wall, we stopped.

"What now?" Connor asked. He shined the light across the wall. It was solid.

I didn't know. Is this where the girls were? I listened and thought maybe, for a second, that I heard a bear growl. That would prove my theory that we'd come back around to where we began. Which meant that there was a door nearby since we'd come in through one.

I tried to orient myself. If we'd walked to the left, that meant the door was just a few feet away.

"Connor," I said, determined to find the door. "Shine that flashlight over here."

There was no answer from my friend. I swung around.

"Connor! No!" Blake's hand was sticking out from the center of the wall. Connor was gripping the light in one hand and being dragged by Blake by the other.

I dove forward to catch his feet as the spirit of Blake pulled Connor's arm through the solid wall.

His front foot moved quickly, and by the time I'd reached his back leg, he was gone.

Connor was gone! That was not how the story was supposed to go! And he had taken the flashlight with him, which meant I was alone and in the dark.

Shivers struck me hard. I couldn't stop shaking. I thought I might be sick. What was I going to do?

"Hang tight, Nate," I said out loud to myself. "Be brave like Connor was. Use what you know." My mind was blank. I tried talking to myself some more. "There's a door. Find it."

I took a deep breath. Which way had we first come in? I closed my eyes since it was dark anyway. Yes…to the left. I reached my hands out toward the wall and ran my fingertips along the smooth surface at about the height where a doorknob might be.

It was a little farther than I remembered, but once I found it, I felt hopeful that I was on the right track.

I swung open that hidden door near the bear display and stepped into the mammals' hall.

It was brighter than I remembered. There were small security lights on the floor and an eerie bluish glow from the grizzly bear exhibit.

I stepped toward the display. There was no way I'd heard a bear growl from inside the passage. The bear was as still as a statue, standing on its rear legs, just like when we'd first come in. There was no movement in the habitat.

The display looked just like it did for regular tourists on a normal day. There was no sign that that grizzly had ever been "alive."

"Connor!" I shouted his name, looking all around the hall and into every display. When there was no answer, I tried, "Bella! Emily!"

The only sound I heard was the ticking of my watch, which bugged me. Every second that passed meant that my friends were closer to staying in the museum forever. I tapped my foot and stared into the bear habitat, as if somehow that bear was going to show me what I needed to do.

Oh, wait!

I didn't know what to do, but I knew who to ask!

I dropped to my knees and pulled out the Scaremaster's journal.

The book fell open to the first page.

The Scaremaster's story was still there. I quickly scanned it. Nothing had changed since we'd left the storage room and it still said "The End" at the bottom of the page.

I dug in the bottom of my bag for the pencil.

I wrote the first thing that popped into my head.

Bring back my friends!

That felt bold and brave, like what the old Nate—the one who wasn't afraid of scary movies or stories—might have written.

The Scaremaster wrote back in his scratchy handwriting.

Okay.

"Okay"? That was too easy. He was going to bring them back just like that? Great!

I looked up to see if he was going to drop them right in front of me. That would have been nice.

But it was the Scaremaster's story, and he was writing it as we went along. A moment later, when my friends hadn't magically reappeared, I checked the book again. This time, he had a question for me and it wasn't nice at all.

Which friend would you like?

Oh, so uncool. What was I supposed to do? I quickly wrote:

All of them.

Pick one.

This was impossible! How could I save one friend and not the others? But I remembered that it was Connor who had been saying we could change the ending of the story. He'd seemed so determined that it could happen. If I had him back, then maybe we could work together to get the girls.

I wrote down his name:

Connor Fletcher

The Scaremaster wrote:

Done.

I half expected Connor to be standing next to me a second later, but again, he wasn't.

In fact, I looked around the hall and didn't see him at all.

where is he?

We're going to play a scary game first. Nate's Nightmare Hide-and-Seek.

I was so mad. I was going to tell the Scaremaster a few things about how I felt about this game he was playing, but then, as I raised the pencil, I heard a bang.

It sounded like a fist on glass, and it took me a moment to figure out where it was coming from.

I found Connor. He was inside the grizzly bear display.

The bear was no longer stuffed and frozen. He was on the prowl now, huffing and growling behind Connor, who was slamming his fists on the glass to get my attention.

He looked back over at the bear, then at me. Then, as Blake had done earlier, Connor seemed to notice something to the side of the display case. He nodded in that direction, then reached into his pocket.

I searched for a way to break the glass and set him free. The only thing I had that was even a little heavy was the Scaremaster's journal. I slammed the book against the glass repeatedly, but nothing happened.

I was furious. The Scaremaster had tricked me. He hadn't brought back any of my friends. At least not safely. He'd made everything so much worse.

Connor pressed a hand to the glass.

"How do I save you?" I shouted.

He cupped his ear as if to say that he couldn't hear.

I yelled it again.

Connor glanced back at the bear again. It seemed to be stalking him, and we both knew he had to protect himself. He had to get away.

Connor slammed his hand against the glass again, and this time, I noticed that in his palm was a plastic wrapper.

He wanted me to see it.

I leaned in. "Is that the gummy dinosaurs?" I asked out loud, even though he couldn't hear me.

He smashed the wrapper against the glass again and gave me a strong and steady look. The bear charged the glass, and Connor ducked away, dashing toward the side of the display and out of the frame.

I looked down at the habitat's grassy ground. Connor had dropped the gummy candy wrapper. It was empty.

What did that mean? What was he trying to tell me? And when had he eaten the gummies?

I thought about all my questions for a long moment before the bear started slamming on the glass again.

Then it came to me!

I didn't know how to save him or Bella or Emily, but now I knew where to go.

Connor was gone, but still, I shouted, as if he might be able to hear me, "I'll meet you at the dinosaurs."

Chapter Eight

The Hall of Dinosaurs had its own floor. The exhibits took up the entire fourth floor of the museum. I got out my map. I had to figure out which way to go and get to the exhibit in the shortest possible time. I missed Emily in more ways than one.

There were several display areas. To one side was a place where paleontologists had re-created dinosaur skeletons. When I'd first looked at the map at home, I was excited to check those displays out. Our class was supposed to go on a morning tour with an expert. I hoped my friends and I would be there. We had to be there!

In the other direction was the Dino Lab, where students could pretend to be on a fossil dig. There were plastic bones hidden in a large sandbox. We'd get a chance to uncover the bones, figure out which kind of dinosaur they belonged to, then, in small groups, work together to build several different skeletons.

Between the two exhibit areas was one of those big movie theaters with huge screens. There was a dinosaur history film that some of the kids in my class thought would be boring, but I couldn't wait to see it.

Again, I hoped we'd be back with the group in time.

This nightmare had to end. And now I was the hero who had to end it. I'd never been a hero before. That was as scary as anything the Scaremaster could've planned.

I pulled the Scaremaster's book out of my bag and opened it. There was nothing new on the page. I wrote:

Which way?

The Scaremaster made me mad when he wrote:

Prepare to disappear. Blake is waiting for his last new friend.

That just wasn't cool at all.

I wrote:

Not going to happen.

I was angry when I closed the book.

My best friend had left me a clue about the dinosaurs, so I decided to head straight to them. The exhibit was huge. On the map, the description said proudly that the Hall of Dinosaurs was fourteen thousand square feet. I wasn't sure how big my house was, but fourteen thousand of anything seemed like a lot. I decided it was too big an area to run everywhere. I had to narrow my search.

"Connor!" I shouted. Then, "Emily! Bella!" I even tried, "Blake!"

The ghost was silent.

I had to get moving, so I asked myself, *What would be Blake's favorite dinosaur?*

T. rex, of course. That was everyone's favorite.

I checked my map. The *Tyrannosaurus rex* was in the center of the display hall. We'd learned in class that its name meant "tyrant lizard" and that the T. rex was the largest meat-eating dinosaur. I knew from my own reading that its massive four-foot-long jaw was designed for bone-crushing action.

I didn't know what I'd do if the T. rex came to life like the bears and birds. If that happened, there was a good chance I'd be a ghost in the blink of an eye. But it felt right to start there. Crossing my fingers in the hope that I'd find my friends, I took off running.

Whoa! When I got to the display, I was shocked. The T. rex was enormous. And there wasn't just one. There were three of the predators side by side. The display showed how they grew from a baby T. rex to a ginormous one.

"Why can't I be on a tour instead of a rescue mission?" I moaned to myself. I had no time to look or read the signs.

It seemed like maybe the T. rex was a wrong first choice. "Hey, guys? Where are you?!" I kept focused on the idea that I was living inside the Scaremaster's story and I could change the ending. But to change it, I had to find my friends.

I began backing up, away from the amazing display. Suddenly, I stepped in something smushy. It felt like gum.

I reached down to pull the gunk off my shoe. The blob was orange and sticky. I grabbed an end of it, and then I realized what I'd stepped in. It wasn't gum. It was gummy. A gummy dinosaur.

My shoe had squished the corner, but the dinosaur was still recognizable as a stegosaurus. That's the one with armored plates down its back and spikes on its tail. I checked the map and figured out which way to go.

"Thanks, Connor," I shouted into the air. My own voice echoed back. From wherever he was, Connor was helping me change the Scaremaster's story. I felt more hopeful than I had since Bella disappeared. Working together, the four of us could stop the Scaremaster.

I took off at top speed.

Past the raptors and pterodactyl, I found a mighty stegosaurus. It was paired with an ankylosaurus. That was the one called a "living tank" because of all its armor. While the fossils were awesome, none of my friends were in the exhibit area. It was disappointing, and I was starting to worry that I was too late.

I made a careful search in case there were other clues. I looked up high, near the top of the display cases, then low along the line of the floor.

A green gummy near the stegosaurus's front left toe caught my eye.

I hurried to get it.

It took me a second to recognize the brachiosaurus. Its neck was folded and stuck back on itself. The gummy was also covered with pocket lint.

"You rock, Connor," I said out loud.

A quick look at the map and off I went, running to the sauropod display, where a huge brachiosaurus took up most of the exhibit. Its tail reached from one wall of the display room to the other.

Near the end of that massive tail, I found dino gummy number three. I immediately knew that the Scaremaster had my friends over by the velociraptors. He was moving them around the displays faster than I could run.

If it wasn't for Connor's clues, I'd never even be close. As it was, I was starting to give up hope. Would I ever catch up? And what would I do once I did find them? What shape would they be in?

I was getting tired of running and scared that my whole hero fantasy wasn't going to work out. What would Mr. Steinberg say when four of his students were missing in the morning? All our parents would be devastated. I bet that even Connor's brothers would miss him.

I didn't want the last anyone heard about us to be a depressing report on the nightly news.

Thinking of our families gave me strength. I took a deep breath and carried on. I was going to find them. The Scaremaster was going down.

At the velociraptors, I found the next gummy that took me to an iguanodon, and from there, the last gummy brought me back to the place I started: the T. rex.

I stood at the base of the huge skeleton display, as close as I could to the T. rexes without setting off the alarm. There was a red velvet rope around the three dinosaurs, so I used that as my boundary.

I screamed the names of my friends. There was no answer.

The Scaremaster might play this game forever. I didn't know when it would end. He'd keep moving my friends and I'd keep chasing them. But now there were no more gummy candies for clues. There'd only been five different kinds in the package.

I was seriously considering going back to where my classmates were sleeping and waking up Mr. Steinberg. But how would I explain what was going on?

I opened the Scaremaster's journal and wrote:

I played your game.
Now, where are they?

This game is not over. Look up.

"Oh, good grief," I muttered, raising my eyes to the largest T. rex fossils.

I should have been surprised when the bones began to creak and shimmy. But I wasn't. This was still the Scaremaster's game. I knew what was coming, so I didn't wait for the most ferocious dinosaur from the Cretaceous period to attack me. I took off running.

The T. rex stretched his bones and broke free from the platform base. The smaller T. rexes didn't move, so that was a positive. Still, when Big T. rex stepped over the velvet cord around the exhibit, I was terrified.

He chased after me, waving his short T. rex arms and gnashing his savage teeth. I'd read that a T. rex could eat five hundred pounds of meat in one bite. I'd be an appetizer!

I wasn't very good at PE. I barely passed the state tests. How could I outrun a T. rex? When the Scaremaster called the game "Nate's Nightmare Hide-and-Seek," he wasn't kidding.

I led the dinosaur through the same route that I'd taken when I was following the gummy trail. Stegosaurus, brachiosaurus, velociraptor, iguanodon, and then we went out of the Hall of Dinosaurs and past the movie theater.

The entire next wing was the interactive dig area. A sign announced: *Be a Paleontologist for the Day.*

Normally, that sounded great. But right now, I was being pursued by a hungry dinosaur while searching for friends who may or may not have already been turned to ghosts.

I ducked through a doorway that was far too small for the dinosaur. In a large room, surrounded by several small classrooms, was a big sand pit. This was the actual "dig." A sign said that fake dinosaur bones were hidden just under the surface in the oversized sandbox.

The T. rex slammed through the wall like a cartoon character, leaving a massive T. rex–shaped hole. I dodged past the sand pit and ran into a classroom.

He crashed in through the window. There was nowhere to hide, so I ran toward the dinosaur, dipping down to slide under him as I made my escape, out of the classroom and back toward the center of the display area.

I hurried to the sand pit. It was a huge square that filled the central part of the room. The walls of the pit were clear so that teachers could observe what was going on, but they were also slick so no one could climb in or out. I didn't see a door, but there had to be one for the students.

I considered searching, but then I thought, *There's no roof on the sandbox.* If the T. rex just leaned over one of those open walls, I'd be trapped. Like a mouse in a box. Or in this case, Nate in a box.

The T. rex was facing me now.

The farther back I pushed toward the sandbox, the more I knew that I was in trouble. There was nowhere left to go. I could hurry into another classroom, if I was fast enough. But the T. rex broke down the last wall easily. He could take them all down. Sooner or later, he'd get me.

I glanced at the entry where I'd come in. I could run that way, try to make a break for the stairs.

Maybe I should go down to another floor? What would I do then? Where could I hide?

The employee tunnel behind the bears might be a safe spot, but I wasn't sure I could find that hidden door again.

My mind was flooded with possibilities for escape. None of them were good. And in every scenario I imagined, I got eaten by the possessed skeleton of a T. rex at the end of the chase.

The monster gave a hollow growl that came from the center of his open bones. His jaw snapped open, and in a flash, he bent toward me.

I dodged his jaw as he tried to bite off my head.

I ducked when he made a stab for my arm with those deadly fangs. My back was up against the sandbox now.

The T. rex lowered his head.

I got ready to run, not sure where I'd go, but knowing I had to try to survive. Hopefully, if I kept moving, the Scaremaster would eventually get tired of torturing me with his gigantic pet.

The T. rex was faster than I anticipated, and his sharp teeth came within striking distance. I dropped to the floor in time, and he ended up biting the side of the sandbox.

When he stepped back to reset for a new attack, I got up to make a run for it. But I didn't get far. I couldn't see behind me but someone, or many people, were lifting me up all at once.

I was hauled over the sandbox wall.

And dropped right into the middle of the dirt.

Chapter Nine

I struggled to stand. I kicked and flailed as my feet slipped in the sand.

The sand was hard-packed on top, but I knew it went deep since bones were planted below the surface for the activity. On a normal museum visit, kids would dig under the sand, like a real paleontologist would at an excavation.

"No!" I screamed as I found my footing. This was not going to be the way it ended. I was not going to let the Scaremaster feed me to a T. rex.

"Nate, stop wiggling. You're getting sand in my eyes."

That voice sure sounded like Emily, but there was no way that could be true. I'd looked in the sandbox when I'd first entered the room. No one was in there.

I stopped thrashing and looked up. Somehow,

Emily, Bella, and Connor were all in the sandbox with me.

The dinosaur slammed his head against the outer wall of the sand pit.

"Not too bright, is he?" Bella remarked. "We should have been eaten right after the Scaremaster dropped us here."

"How long ago was that?" I asked.

"About a second ago," Emily told me.

"That's why I didn't see you when I came in." I quickly turned to Connor. "Thanks for the clues."

"You're welcome." Connor grinned. "It was actually Blake's idea." With a thumb, Connor pointed to the ghost, who was now standing behind the T. rex, distracting the dinosaur by pulling on his tail.

The T. rex turned around but didn't see Blake there. Apparently, dinosaurs couldn't see ghosts. Blake stuck out his tongue at the beast.

The T. rex growled in the ghost's general direction.

"I've been spending time with Blake," Bella said. "Since I was the *first* to disappear." The way she said it reminded me that Bella really liked being the first at anything. Even if it was the first at being grabbed by a ghost kid with the Scaremaster's journal. "He's nice." She waved at Blake as he ripped off a bone from the T. rex's tail, giving us another minute to talk. "The Scaremaster dropped me into Blake's room. He has a little closet that's all set up like a real bedroom."

"Blake wished to live in the museum," Emily told me. "But he regrets it now. Ghost life isn't nearly as great as he imagined."

"He misses cookies," Connor said. "And seeing movies."

Apparently, after they each disappeared, they were taken to Blake's "home."

"He's seen the dinosaur show a million times," Bella said.

"It's great the first three hundred times," Blake replied. He tore off two more tail bones.

The others laughed. I didn't. What was going on? While I was running around looking for them, was it possible that they'd all become best friends?

This was so weird. And I wasn't sure I trusted the ghost as much as my friends seemed to.

"Well," I said, "being friends is fine, but we are about to get eaten by a giant carnivorous dinosaur!"

"I'm doing my best here to distract him." Blake

jabbed one of the T. rex's toe bones. "You should make a run for it."

The T. rex snarled to the air, chomped his teeth, then gnarled toward the sandbox.

"There's no time to run," I said, feeling panic rise in my chest. "If we don't do something fast, we're going to join Blake, forever!"

"That's the idea," Blake admitted as the dinosaur stalked us like prey. "The Scaremaster said he'd arrange it."

That statement was so odd, especially since he'd just been trying to save us. What was Blake really up to?

The others were thrilled that Blake was working to distract the T. rex. They thought he was helping us so we could escape the sand pit. But when we looked, we couldn't find the door. It was as if the sand pit was sealed shut.

I could hear the ticking of my watch, warning us that time was almost up.

"I have an idea." Emily began digging in the sand. She pulled out a large gray-colored fake fossil and swung it like a baseball bat.

"That's an allosaurus femur," Blake told her.

"We need weapons," Emily told us. "We're going to attack."

"Uh, it's a T. rex," I said, not wanting to be a downer, but really? This was her plan? We were going to swing a bunch of plastic bones at an attacking T. rex?

"You got a better idea, Nate?" Emily challenged me.

The T. rex snarled.

"Nope," I admitted, and started digging in the sand. I found a triceratops horn.

Connor got a sauropod claw.

Bella was the big winner with a sharp T. rex tooth. It was almost a foot long. "Is this yours?" she taunted the T. rex, who was snarling at us.

Blake couldn't hold him off much longer. We were armed and ready.

"Okay, Blake," Emily said. "Let him loose!"

When Blake stepped back from the T. rex, I swore I heard him laugh.

I looked at my friends. None of them seemed to notice the echoing chuckle. They were all ready and poised with their weapons.

"When the T. rex breaks through the sand pit

wall, smack him hard to try to break him apart," Emily told us.

I was the big killjoy. "What's that going to do? He's possessed. His bones will just pop back up into place, and he'll regenerate."

Bella agreed with Emily. "We are going to smash him into a zillion bones so we can break out of here and get away."

I'd already had that fantasy in my imagination. It ended with me getting eaten.

There had to be another way.

"Wait!" I shouted. "What about the Scaremaster?"

"Huh?" Connor turned to me. "What about him?"

"You said we need to change the story," I reminded him. "The T. rex is being controlled by the Scaremaster. If we go after the Scaremaster and his story, then that should stop the T. rex."

"That's a terrible plan," Blake said, now next to the T. rex. He'd moved, closer to the sand pit. "Smacking at the dinosaur with fake bones is the best idea." He flashed a smile at Emily.

She grinned back.

The T. rex was just standing there. I didn't

understand why he hadn't attacked us already. Something was off.

Blake said, "Attack the dinosaur. Come on. Smack him like a piñata."

I immediately understood that was exactly what we *shouldn't* do.

"Blake's tricking us," I told my friends. "He still wants us to be ghosts like him. And that means we need to get eaten by the T. rex."

"That's not true," Bella told me. I noticed she'd gotten her second shoe back. Blake must have given it to her after he dropped it. "He wants to be our friend."

"Friends forever," Blake said, agreeing.

"Friends *forever*," I said. "*Forever!* Don't you see? That's how the Scaremaster's story ends." I turned to Connor. Surely, he'd be on my side. "We're still in the story. Nothing's changed." My eyes flitted between Blake and the T. rex. In my mind, they were obviously linked. It was the Scaremaster's story, but Blake was somehow controlling the dinosaur. That was why we hadn't been ghostified yet.

"You're just jealous," Bella told me. "We have a new friend. We've been spending time with Blake. We like him."

"He wants you to like him!" I insisted. "He wants us to stay here."

"Not you," Blake corrected me. "I like Bella, Connor, and Emily." Blake pinched his lips together. His voice was low. I didn't think the others heard him. "But you just aren't as fun as them." And as he said it, I was magically pulled out of the sand pit, as if by imaginary strings, leaving my friends behind.

"Can't you see what is happening?" I shouted as I was hauled backward and stuffed into one of the classrooms. The door slammed shut. This was terrible. I tried the knob, knowing before I even twisted it that Blake had somehow locked the door. I could see what was happening outside through the glass. My friends were swinging their weapons at the T. rex while Blake stood, smiling, in a corner. I had to stop this!

I looked around the classroom. This was one of the rooms where teams would go to put together the bones they'd found and make a dinosaur skeleton. There were long tables. Diagrams of several dinosaurs. I opened a cabinet and found construction paper, glue, and some rope. There were instructions on how to make dinosaur pictures to take home.

The worst part was that there were no door keys hanging on a hook and nothing I could use to break out of the room.

I didn't know if my friends could hear me, but I had to make contact. They wouldn't be able to hear through the glass, so I was determined to crack it.

I slammed the plastic triceratops horn against the glass, over and over until a small crack appeared. Then I yelled through the crack, "Blake wants friends. You were dropped in the sand pit so the T. rex could gobble you up. If we don't do something, you'll all live here with him."

"You're ridiculous. That doesn't make sense! Connor yelled back. "Blake's helping us."

"No! Blake's controlling the T. rex. It's all a trick." I looked around the room once more for another way out. There wasn't one. I took my triceratops horn and started slamming it against the window again.

The window finally shattered into a hole big enough for me to squeeze through. I carefully climbed out through the shards of glass, just as my friends slammed their weapons into the T. rex skeleton. The T. rex broke apart, and with a giant crash, the bones fell to the floor in a pile.

"See?" Connor said as I ran into the room. "Blake was right. He told us how to defeat the T. rex."

Emily and Bella hugged each other.

I felt the pull of those invisible strings dragging me back. A second later, I was going to be locked in another classroom. That was when I saw the small silver knob of the sand pit door.

I lunged forward, grabbed it, and held on. It felt a little like I was fighting against a tornado. My feet slid along the floor as the spirit of the Scaremaster, or Blake, or something fought me. I gripped the knob tighter and twisted with all my strength.

"Let's go," I told my friends. "Hurry."

I kept twisting, only to realize the knob was turning loosely in my hand. The door wasn't opening. First, I couldn't find the knob, and now that I had found it, it didn't work. This was all some kind of evil, sick game. "Figures," I moaned.

"You're trapped in the pit," I told my friends. "This proves that Blake is the bad guy here."

"It doesn't prove anything. There's no danger," Connor said. He pointed to the pile of fallen T. rex bones. "We have all the time on Earth. Nate, go find a key." He said to Blake, "Come on. Stop fooling around with Nate. He's never really been able to take a joke. No sense of humor."

"This isn't right," I said as the strings that were dragging me back suddenly disappeared. I slumped to the museum floor.

"The Scaremaster has something to say," Blake told me. He'd moved quickly across the room and was now standing above me, smirking.

I stood and faced him. "I hope it's that you're going to live alone." I was angry, and the anger bubbled inside my chest. He was tricking my friends, but they liked him so much that I couldn't convince them that the ghost boy was evil.

I grabbed the Scaremaster's book out of my bag. There was part of the story that was now nagging at me. If we weren't going to be eaten by the T. rex, how were we going to become ghosts in the museum?

What do you want? I scribbled hard with the pencil.

His answer was simple:

Some scientists think the
dinosaurs died when an asteroid
hit the earth. Others blame
changes in climate. There were
sticky tar pits in some regions.
But in the state of Utah, this is
how the dinosaurs died....

Utah? What did I know about dinosaurs in Utah!?

I looked over at my friends and gasped with horror.

The sand beneath them had turned to quicksand.

They were sinking.

Chapter Ten

Blake cheered. He clapped his hands. "This is awesome!"

"No!" I screamed as I ran back to the locked door at the side of the sand pit. I pulled and tugged at the handle. The harder I tried to open the door, the more Blake laughed.

"Do you still think he's on your side?" I asked my friends. They were ankle-deep now and dropping fast. The sand was thick and sticky. It was pulling them down, and the harder they struggled to get free, the more the quicksand grabbed them and tugged.

"Don't move!" I shouted. "It makes it worse."

"Save us," Connor called back. I was about to reply with "How?" but then I realized he was looking at Blake, not me. "The Scaremaster is trying to drown us in the sand pit."

Blake pretended that he couldn't hear. "What?" he called to Connor. "Speak louder."

My voice was getting hoarse from all the shouting, but I did my best to yell back. "He's the one that's making you sink. He's working with the Scaremaster."

"Blake," Emily called out. "Get us out of here!" She was also ignoring me.

Blake looked over at me. The expression on his face was joyful. "I'm going to have three new friends," he cried. "And you'll have none."

Inside the pit, Connor, Emily, and Bella were now in sand that came up to their knees.

It was Bella who first realized that I was the good guy, not Blake. "Nate, do something!" she cried. "I don't want to be a ghost in the museum." She cast her eyes at Blake and said, "Sorry. But I don't."

"We'll be together," Blake told her. "We can see the planetarium show as many times as you want. And we can prank the visitors with that attacking bird trick I did. You should have seen how scared you all were." He grasped his belly while he laughed. "It's going to be so much fun when we're all living here." Blake stopped laughing and said, "It'll be a sleepover party every night."

Connor and Emily finally understood.

"Blake," Connor said, "we can come visit you. We don't have to live here."

That was a good try. Connor was still the best at those convincing arguments. Only this time, it didn't work.

Blake waved his hands, and my friends sank down to their waists in the sand.

"The change won't hurt," Blake assured them. "You stop breathing for a moment when the sand covers your face, but then it's over."

He sounded like a doctor giving a shot.

"When you open your eyes again, you'll be just like me," he finished, as if that were a good thing.

"Help, Nate!" Emily shouted. "Don't let him do this."

I didn't know how to stop it. All I had was the map, the Scaremaster's journal, a pencil, and some licorice.

Licorice.

Okay, so that was a place to start.

I reached into the shopping bag and pulled out the candy.

"There's no time for a snack," Connor told me. His voice cracked with stress.

"I'm not hungry," I replied over my shoulder as

I ran back to the classroom where Blake had trapped me. He couldn't trap me in there again because the glass was shattered, but I wondered if he'd drag me off to another room. Between Blake and the Scaremaster, anything was possible.

I stopped before climbing over the broken glass and stared back at Connor. I opened my eyes wide, and thought hard thoughts, hoping to send him a signal. I did not believe in mind reading; that would be silly. But I did believe that Connor and I had been friends for such a long time that maybe he could figure out what I was doing and help.

"Hey, Blake," I heard him say as I saw the sticky sand engulf his waist. "Tell us about the"— he stalled for a beat—"kinds of pranks we can play on museum visitors. That sounds fun."

"Yeah," Emily said, getting the point. "The bird thing was terrifying."

"I know," Blake said with a chuckle. "I've only done that one once before. I like to work with the bears. They're my favorite. Teddy—that's what I call the big grizzly—he's such a jokester. I can't wait for you to meet him. Did you see how he scared Connor?"

Connor nodded. "I was terrified. Especially when I was inside the display, behind the glass."

Blake nodded. "Teddy can wiggle just an ear. Or one little finger. Or inch closer to the display glass while no one is looking....The tourists go nuts, wondering if something changed. It's hysterical."

This was working. My friends weren't sinking anymore, and I could move more quickly without feeling like Blake was watching my every move.

"And the rats in with the birds of prey—how cool was that?" Blake continued. "None of them were hurt, of course. All the animals are friends. It was all staged for your benefit. But it was great, wasn't it?"

While Blake rambled on, I crept over the shards of glass and back into the classroom. Inside that cabinet, I'd seen some rope. It wasn't a lot, but it would be enough. Tucking the rope into my shopping bag, I slipped back into the main area, ducked behind the pile of T. rex bones, and opened the licorice package. It wasn't the candy I wanted. It was the book of knots.

Just because I knew that the figure eight was the best knot for climbing didn't mean I'd ever made one. I wondered if there was a better knot for what I had planned. Maybe the Palomar, the one Connor mentioned when we first found the book, was the right one for this? It was meant for fishing after all, and I was going fishing for my friends.

I flipped through the pages of the small book and found the one I needed.

It was a timber hitch. This was a knot that could be used to drag a tree log, so it should be strong enough to drag three kids out of a sand pit. I looped the end of the rope around my own waist and tied three small knots for gripping into the long part of the rope. My friends could hold on, and I would walk backward, pulling them out of the sand.

I made the knot around me tight. After that, I quickly threw one end over the side of the sand pit where Emily could grab it.

"Grab a knot and hang on tight," I told her. "Don't let go."

She found a place to hold on, then pushed the rope to where Connor and Bella could also reach. They all had to drag their hands out of the sand to get the knots. That little movement pulled them down more into the sand than if they'd stayed still.

I moved back to where the rope was tight, then pulled back. I grunted and groaned, but the quicksand was like cement. It was hard-packed, thick, and pasty. The sand wouldn't let my friends go.

Blake was laughing hysterically now. The moment I'd thrown the rope into the pit, he'd stopped talking about museum pranks. To my surprise, he hadn't tried to stop my rescue mission. Now I understood why. He knew this wouldn't work. The rope was too thin and was already fraying. And I had to admit, I was too weak to pull three people out of quicksand.

To Blake, this was just a huge joke. And the punch line was that my friends would become ghosts like him.

Suddenly, Connor dropped the rope. The sand had reached his neck. He gasped for air. "Nate," he choked out my name. "Change the story."

Bella's tooth fossil was on the sand. After she dropped her rope knot, she still had a hand free. It was awkward, but she managed to throw the fake fossil at me over the edge of the pit. I caught it and ran a finger over the fake T. rex tooth. It wasn't very sharp.

"Stab the book!" Emily said just as the sand

touched the bottom of her lip. She spit some out of her mouth.

My hands were shaking when I pulled the Scaremaster's book out of the shopping bag.

Using the tooth as a stake, I stabbed at the book's cover. It didn't make a dent. Instead, bits of plastic broke off the fake fossil. "It's not working," I cried, glancing into the sand pit to see that the sand was now up to Connor's mouth as well. Only Bella seemed to have her whole head free. This was probably the first time she wasn't "first."

"You're too late," Blake jeered at me. "When we're friends, hanging out all day and night in the museum, you won't ever be invited to visit, Nate. Not ever!"

I didn't even look at him. Stabbing at the book was getting nowhere, so I opened the cover and tried stabbing at the pages.

"The book is made of the toughest paper I've ever seen," I complained.

"Glurg," responded Connor.

That wasn't good. I spun to face him. He was breathing through his nose now because the sand was covering his mouth.

I needed something sharper to stab at the pages. But what?

"Glugggg!" repeated Connor in a throaty growl.

Don't ask how that translated in my head to "tooth" but it did. I was sitting near a huge pile of dinosaur bones. In that pile was one of the sharpest things in the entire prehistoric world. The T. rex had tried to bite me with his teeth, and now I was going to use them to save my friends.

I grabbed one of the T. rex teeth from the fossil pile and held it in my hand. It was huge. Nearly a foot long.

"Got it," I called back to Connor.

I was careful not to touch the sharpest part, grabbing the back of the tooth and raising it like a spike.

"Good-bye, Scaremaster," I yelled, gathering my energy to slam the tooth through the possessed journal's cover. I took a deep breath.

A roar swelled behind me. I paused, feeling heat on my neck. A clinking noise filled the hall, echoing all around me. I wished I hadn't turned to look right then because it might have been over if I'd just stabbed the book.

Another roar filled the hall as the T. rex's bones clicked back into place one after another. The T. rex was rebuilding himself, and I had no doubt that he was going to want his tooth.

"You aren't going to change the story," Blake challenged me. "The Scaremaster promised *me* a happy ending."

The T. rex gathered himself together. Looking up, I could see the gaping hole where the tooth I held should have been.

I couldn't let him have that tooth.

There was a strange pull on the fossil. It felt like a magnet was trying to tear the tooth from my hand and suck it back into that giant T. rex's mouth.

I held firm.

The T. rex gnashed his jaw directly over my head. I was certain that I was going to be the next ghost in the museum. Me first, then my friends.

There was only one thing to do. I closed my eyes and tried not to think about the fact that in about ten seconds I was going to be dinosaur food.

I raised my hands and, using every muscle in my body, I slammed that tooth down. It was so sharp that it easily pierced the Scaremaster's journal cover and dug through the pages.

For a moment, it was completely quiet, and then there was so much noise. Crashing, shattering, and screams. I couldn't see where any of it was coming from, and I didn't know whether I'd changed the story.

I tried to see into the sand pit, but all I could make out was sand. Were my friends underneath it? Was it over? Had I lost?

My last thought before everything started spinning and the room went dark was:

Am I a ghost?

Chapter Eleven

When I opened my eyes, I was lying on a hard floor. I did a mental scan of my body. Toes, check. Knees, still there. Hips, belly, shoulders, neck, head, yep, I still had all those parts too. The good news was that I was all in one piece.

I blinked open my eyes and stared at a dark ceiling.

Slowly, I sat up.

"That's strange," I muttered to myself.

I was in my sleeping bag, in the room with my classmates. They were all still asleep. I rubbed my eyes.

Had it all been a dream? Was there really no ghost? No Scaremaster?

I yawned, blinked hard, then looked over to Connor's bag. It was empty. There was no sign that he'd been there at all.

Slowly, so as not to wake Mr. Steinberg or the other kids in my class, I stood up.

In a whispered voice, I called, "Connor?" Maybe he'd fallen asleep somewhere else in the room? That didn't make sense, but I was nervous that the only one who'd been saved when I stabbed the journal was me.

Where was Connor?

His voice came from across the room, near a case of purple crystals. "Nate...hurry..." He held up a book.

I could see it was the Scaremaster's journal and the T. rex tooth was piercing the center.

Now I was certain. This hadn't been a dream.

I tiptoed around other sleeping bags, toward Connor.

When I reached him, he whispered in my ear, "Follow me."

We left the room and headed to the broad staircase. I was walking behind him, which gave me time to take a good look at Connor's body. Blake had been blurred along the edges. Connor looked totally solid.

"Are you a ghost?" I asked as we climbed the steps to the dinosaur exhibit on the fourth floor.

He turned back toward me. "No," he said simply.

"Am I?" I asked, pinching my own arms as I said it.

"No," he said, again without explaining anything.

"The girls?" I asked. "Emily and Bella?"

"Alive," he told me. "Come on. You're walking too slow." With his long legs, Connor leapt up the stairs two at a time. I struggled to keep up.

"Where are we going?" I asked. "What's going on? What happened at the end of the story?" I was being stubborn and stopped. "I'm not moving until you explain a few things."

With a mighty sigh, he paused at the top of the stairway, in front of the dinosaur movie theater. "You did it, Nate," he said at last. "You saved us."

"So why did I wake up on the floor downstairs with everyone else?" This was so confusing.

"I don't know," Connor told me. "Emily, Bella, and I popped out of the sand pit, but we were still in the same room. You were gone."

"How'd you find me?" I had so many questions. I could tell Connor didn't want to waste time answering them all. He was talking really fast to spit out the information and get me moving again.

"I went back through everywhere the Scaremaster's story had taken us tonight. The dinosaur fossils, the bears, the birds, and finally down to where we started. If you hadn't been in your sleeping bag, I was going to the gift shop next."

I reached out and gave him a small punch in the arm. "Good thinking," I said. "It was like you read the Scaremaster's story backward."

"Right," Connor told me. "Except for one thing…" As he said that, I heard the growl. It was mighty and echoed through the dinosaur exhibit to where we were standing.

Connor grabbed my hand. "The Scaremaster's story isn't over yet."

"What are you talking about?" I asked as he took off running. "I stabbed the book. You got out of the sand. And I woke up at the beginning. What more could there be?"

He held up the book and shook it in my direction. "The epilogue."

An epilogue was the part at the end of the book that was like a last comment. The last bit that said what happened after the story seemed to be over.

"Epilogue?" I questioned as we arrived back in the room with the sand pit. I shook my head. "Oh!" I got what Connor meant. He was right. There was one last little bit of the Scaremaster's story left.

Emily and Bella were standing near the pit, each holding a plastic bone from the pit. They were swinging those weapons at a re-formed T. rex skeleton.

The T. rex roared.

"Help," Emily squealed. "We've been holding this thing off since you disappeared."

"We sent Connor to get you," Bella told me. "You defeated the Scaremaster before. Do it again, Nate. And hurry."

It was then that I noticed Blake. He was sitting on a table in one of the classrooms, swinging his feet and watching the battle through the large window. It was a different classroom from where I'd broken the window. That room was still trashed. Nothing was fixed. The hole in the wall from when the T. rex had chased me was still there too.

Blake smiled and waved casually. He looked as if he was winning. His face was so calm, as if he knew that we'd soon be living with him after all.

"You're going to lose, Blake," I called out.

I was angry with him for all he'd done. If he

thought we'd be friends with him after this, he was crazy. My blood was boiling as I looked down for something to throw. I didn't see anything right away, but then, recalling how easily he'd broken pieces off the T. rex, I let the girls distract the sharp-toothed beast while I snuck under his open belly. I went around to the back and broke a fossil off his tail.

I was surprised. It came off easily.

I looked up to find that Blake was smiling at me through that glass window.

I'd never felt so much anger before. Everything he'd done that night and how he'd led us through the Scaremaster's story had made me furious. I threw that bit of tail at the classroom window. The glass shattered.

Blake seemed shocked that I was strong enough to break the window.

Honestly, I was too.

I grabbed another tail fossil and hurled it. And another. And another.

"Wait!" Connor reached out and stopped me from ripping off the entire tail. "That's it, Nate. You really are a genius."

I didn't feel like one. I just felt like a ball of raw emotion.

"I know how to get rid of the T. rex and defeat the Scaremaster at the same time," Connor said. He asked Emily, "Is the pit still quicksand?"

He explained that if the room hadn't been fixed, then maybe everything was exactly how it had been at the end of the story. Only the people had been saved. Nothing else had changed.

"I'll check the pit," Bella told us, sacrificing her shoe again. She tossed it into the sand where it immediately sank. "Quicksand," she reported, then went back to battle with Emily. They both ducked as the T. rex opened his cracking jaw and snapped at them.

"Break it up," Connor hollered. He rushed under the T. rex to where I was and started grabbing off chunks of fossil tail. "The Scaremaster said the dinosaurs in Utah died in quicksand. This one's going to die that way too." He lobbed two big bones over the wall of the sand pit, where they were sucked under the sand.

We dismantled the giant dinosaur as fast as we could. One of us would distract him, while the others tore off anything we could grab. Altogether a T. rex could weigh nine tons, but piece by piece, it was pretty light.

The hardest part was avoiding the head. That snapping jaw was dangerous and scary.

We pulled his body fossils off one by one and threw them into the quicksand. The bones disappeared under the goopy sand and didn't reappear.

Finally, we got down to the head. Without a neck, it didn't have a way to move around, but it still wasn't going to let us near it. When we got close, the head would roll away, and that massive jaw would snap.

Emily grabbed the plastic femur she'd been using as a weapon. "Cover me," she exclaimed. She leapt forward and set that fake bone like a tent pole in the T. rex's mouth. We could see him struggling against it as the plastic bone held his jaw open.

"Now we move it," Emily said.

It was probably the most dangerous thing I'd done in my whole twelve years. We were fighting an animated T. rex skull that wanted to kill us. His jaw was stuck open, but it wouldn't last long before his strong bite crushed through the plastic bone that Emily had used as a prop.

Each of us grabbed a side of the T. rex skull. It was larger up close than it had seemed when it had been chasing me through the museum.

In the end, it took the four of us and a few of those timber hitch knots with the last of my rope to lob that thing over the side of the sand pit.

The sand gurgled and glopped as it sucked that huge head into the depths and cemented it forever.

Things happened fast after that.

The shattered glass of the classroom began to repair itself. The wall where the T. rex had crashed through started to re-form.

"The quicksand is changing to regular sand," Bella told me.

"That's good news," I said, relieved.

Bella pointed at the Scaremaster's journal. Connor had set it down when we were drowning the T. rex in sand.

"Get rid of that thing, Nate," Bella told me. "Hurry."

I was glad to get rid of the book. In my best storytelling voice, I shouted, "THE END!" and lobbed the book over the side and into the pit.

The Scaremaster's journal landed in the center of the sand pit. The sand began to swirl around the book, like a dusty whirlpool. A moment later, the journal was sucked into the tempest and disappeared.

Chapter Twelve

Blake was sad. "The Scaremaster promised..." he muttered.

He was in the main room with us now, standing by the sand pit. The book was gone and, with it, Blake's dream of having sleepover parties every night with ghost friends.

Emily, Bella, and Connor felt more sympathetic than I did.

"He just wanted someone to hang out with," Emily said. "Nothing wrong with that."

I disagreed. "You can't force people to be your friends."

We left Blake on the fourth floor and snuck down to get back in our sleeping bags. It was nearly morning. The staff was going to wake everyone up soon for the tour of the dinosaur exhibit. I wondered whether the T. rex had rebuilt itself in the great hall. We'd find out soon enough.

"I get what it's like to be lonely," Connor replied. "Even with three brothers, sometimes I feel like that."

Bella said, "Trying to feed new friends to a chomping dinosaur isn't cool."

We went on talking about Blake and what had happened until we reached the second floor, where we had to go separate ways.

"I'm glad we have each other," Emily said. She gave us each a big hug before she and Bella went off toward their sleeping area.

I was exhausted.

Connor and I didn't talk after the girls left us. Walking in silence, we went back to our own sleeping bags and curled up. When Mr. Steinberg woke us, it felt like we'd only been asleep for a minute or two.

I yawned as we went to breakfast.

Connor slept through the dinosaur movie. "Lived it," he said before starting to snore.

I was glad to see the T. rex was back on display, and other than a small piece of gummy brachiosaurus on the floor near the iguanodon, there was no sign of what had happened the night before.

I was on alert. Blake was still in the museum, and

I didn't know if he had any other tricks up his sleeve. But as the day ended, there was no sign of him.

Connor's brother Chris picked us up when it was time to go home. The deal was my mom drove us there, and he'd drive us home.

"How was it?" he asked as he piled our duffel bags into the trunk of his run-down sedan. Chris was nearly twenty and studying biology at the local community college. He looked like a taller, older Connor. Cameron was with him. Cameron was a sophomore in high school.

Charles, a senior, wasn't with them because he was at a soccer game. They all looked alike, just like in the T. rex exhibit with the different size rexes. I couldn't believe that Connor had ever fallen for their story that he wasn't related to them.

"The tour was good," I said. "I got a book about bears."

"We saw a show at the planetarium," Connor told his brothers as the two of us climbed into the backseat.

"That's it?" Cameron asked, turning to look at us over his shoulder.

"Yeah," Connor said, glancing at me. "Was there something else we were supposed to see?"

I caught the side-eye look between Chris and Cameron in the front seats.

"No ghost sightings?" Chris asked. "I mean, we warned you about the kid who lived in the museum."

They were digging for information. I reached out and put a hand on Connor's knee to warn him not to say anything about Blake.

"No, we didn't see any ghosts," I said.

That seemed to throw them off.

"We sent a surprise," Cameron said. "Did you see it?"

I didn't know what they were hinting at. By the look on Connor's face, neither did he.

"Ah man," Chris exclaimed. "Did Mr. S take away your phone?"

"Yes," Connor said, slowly, trying to piece together what his brothers had done.

"A great prank ruined," Chris moaned. He pulled the car around the parking lot and started to head toward my house. "We set up that whole ghost story, even put a video online."

"We knew you'd search for the story," Cameron admitted. "So we made a fake newscast."

"Oh, that," Connor said. "Yeah, I saw it."

"We left it just long enough for you to see it. After a while, we took it down," Cameron admitted. "It was only meant for you."

That explained the partial video that Connor had seen outside the museum store. But it didn't explain anything else that had happened last night.

"Hysterical, right?" Chris said, smacking his hand on the steering wheel. "We had my friend Joe edit the film to make it look like it really came from TV."

"It was scary," Connor admitted. He wrinkled his eyebrows. "Did you talk to the woman at the museum store about the ghost story?"

"What woman?" Cameron asked. "We didn't tell anyone what we were doing. Did someone else make up a ghost story too?"

"Yep," I said. "Ghost stories are very popular at the Natural History Museum."

"We really thought we'd get you with ours," Chris said.

Cameron started to chuckle. "We put a lot of effort into this. We made up the kid, made up the disappearance, and then loaded a video online so that if you wanted to hear more about it, you'd be convinced. Did it work?"

"Did you both stay up all night with spooky nightmares?" Chris asked.

We didn't answer. Connor and I simply looked at each other in confusion.

"Wait. Are you saying there was never a kid called Blake who disappeared in the museum?" Connor asked.

Cameron answered, seriously this time. "No. There was never a kid named Blake."

Chapter Thirteen

"Good morning, students," Mr. Steinberg welcomed us to science class. "I hope you've all completed your homework."

I sat at my assigned desk between Bella and Emily. Connor sat in front of me.

We all pulled out our homework as the bell rang.

Mr. Steinberg came around to collect the papers. "Today, we are going to talk about how the dinosaurs died. Let's see what you learned on our field trip."

Emily reached over and poked me in the arm. She whispered, "We sank a T. rex in quicksand."

Bella heard her and laughed.

Connor leaned back. "Shhh…" We'd sworn each other to secrecy. No one would even believe what had happened to us on the field trip, so we weren't going to talk about it in public. If we did, there was a good chance we'd be branded as crazy.

"There are several theories," Mr. Steinberg began, when suddenly, the classroom door opened.

It was Mrs. Hartford, our principal. "Hate to interrupt," she said, pushing up her glasses and glancing down at her clipboard. "But we have a new student. He's starting school today." She stepped aside so that the new boy could enter. "I hope you will all welcome Blake Turner. Blake just told me he's excited to make some new friends," she said warmly. "And I'm sure he will find them here."

With that, Mrs. Hartford left the room.

"Welcome, Blake," Mr. Steinberg said. "We're glad you can join us. Tell us all a little about yourself."

Blake Turner looked exactly like he had in the museum. He was wearing the same baseball jersey and cap, with the same gray sweatpants.

Mr. Steinberg asked him to remove his hat during class.

I couldn't stop staring at him. As he took off the baseball cap, his head seemed to shimmer a little, like the colors of his hair and skin blurred at the edges.

I gasped.

"I lived on the other side of town," Blake told the class. "My parents move around a lot. They wanted to live closer to the museum."

"We just had our annual field trip to the museum," Mr. Steinberg said. "Have you been there?"

"Many times," Blake admitted. His eyes were glued to mine. Neither of us could look away. "It practically feels like I live there."

"That's great," Mr. Steinberg said. "Let's get you a seat. We were about to talk about the demise of the dinosaurs. I'm sure you'll have a lot to share."

"I think so." Blake nodded. He broke his gaze from mine and gave equally hard stares to Connor, Emily, and Bella.

"Mrs. Hartford spoke of making friends," Mr. Steinberg said. "I'm sure you'll find a nice group right here in this room." There were no empty desks, so he pulled a chair from the side of the room. "Until we get you a desk of your own, you can sit with Nate. I think the two of you will get along really well. Nate can introduce you to Connor, Emily, and Bella."

"Thank you, Mr. Steinberg." Blake grinned as he took a seat next to me.

I leaned back in my chair and tried ignore the way Blake was staring at me.

We'd destroyed the journal, and yet, we'd come to the Scaremaster's ending after all.

Blake and his friends lived happily ever after.

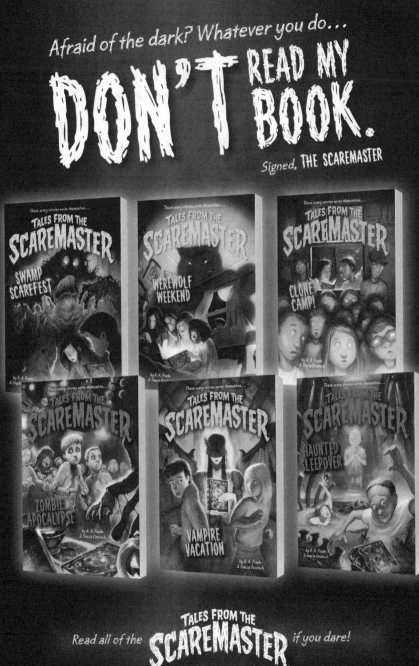

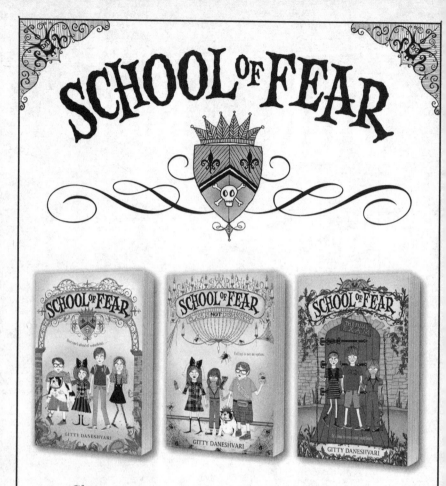

Sharpen your pencils and put on a brave face.
The School of Fear is waiting for YOU!
Will you banish your fears and graduate on time?

IT'S NEVER TOO LATE TO APPLY!

www.EnrollinSchoolofFear.com

 LITTLE, BROWN AND COMPANY
BOOKS FOR YOUNG READERS

Available wherever books are sold.

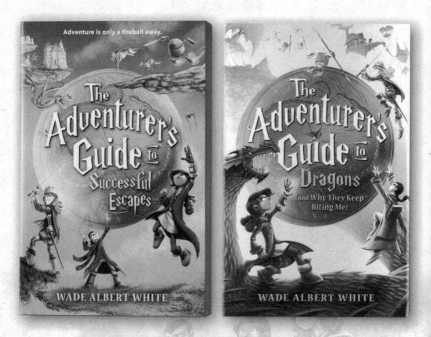
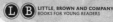